fatherchristmas.con

Jamie Rix is the son of actors Brian Rix and Elspeth Gray. A TV producer in his spare time (*Smith and Jones, KYTV, Harry Hill*), his first children's book, *Grizzly Tales for Gruesome Kids*, was the Smarties Book Prize Children's Choice. Since then he has adapted *Grizzly Tales* and his other collections of cautionary tales, *Ghostly Tales for Ghastly Kids*, *Fearsome Tales for Fiendish Kids* and *More Grizzly Tales for Gruesome Kids*, into an award-winning animation series on CiTV. His other books include *Johnny Casanova* and *The Changing Face of Johnny Casanova* – soon to be an animated series for TV; *The Fire in Henry Hooter*; *The Cool Guide*; and a picture book for younger children called *The Last Chocolate Biscuit*. Married with two grown-up sons, Jamie lives in south London.

Books by the same author

Johnny Casanova

The Changing Face of Johnny Casanova

The Fire in Henry Hooter

fatherchristmas.con

jamie rix

WALKER BOOKS
AND SUBSIDIARIES
LONDON · BOSTON · SYDNEY · AUCKLAND

For my dad

First published 2003 by Walker Books Ltd
87 Vauxhall Walk, London SE11 5HJ

2 4 6 8 10 9 7 5 3 1

Text © 2003 Jamie Rix
Illustrations © 2003 Jason Ford

The right of Jamie Rix to be identified as author
of this work has been asserted by him in accordance
with the Copyright, Designs and Patents Act 1988

This book has been typeset in Sabon, Providence Sans
and Times New Roman

Printed in Great Britain by Cox & Wyman Ltd, Reading, Berkshire

British Library Cataloguing in Publication Data:
a catalogue record for this book is
available from the British Library

ISBN 0-7445-9073-6

www.walkerbooks.co.uk

*If you who own the things people
must have could understand this, you
might preserve yourself... For the quality
of owning freezes you forever into "I,"
and cuts you off forever from the "we."*

John Steinbeck, *The Grapes of Wrath*

CHAPTER ONE

The snow leopard lifted his head out of the ice hole as the noise of exploding steam punctured the still morning air. In the distance a plume of smoke pinpointed a cluster of buildings. The snow leopard set off for home, his red name tag clinking against the buckle on his collar like a single sleigh bell.

The four buildings were huddled tightly together as if to keep out the cold. The smoke snaked upwards from the chimney of a stone cottage that had a low front door, tiny wooden windows and walls thick with thorny Christmas roses. To the left of the cottage across the courtyard stood an L-shaped barn. A steam-driven generator hissed and fumed behind its wooden frame. From inside came a hammering and clanking that filled the North Pole with industrial echoes. This was the factory floor where dreams were made to order. To the right was a row of stables. At the end of these stables, jutting into the yard as far as the barn and completing the rectangle of buildings, was a dark green hut with a corrugated metal roof.

A procession of little men wearing leather shorts called lederhosen and feathered caps scurried out of the back of the factory, their arms laden with toys, and disappeared inside the green hut. Its wooden doors stood ajar, revealing glimpses of gold and orange costumes, and heads as round as pumpkins. Lit by the wicks of oil lamps, short stocky female elves were wrestling with long sheets of wrapping paper and stacking presents onto a twelve-metre sleigh with padded red seats and shiny silver runners.

The snow leopard left a neat line of footprints in the snow as he trotted across the courtyard and nudged open the door to the cottage. At one end of the living room was a sitting area with a favourite armchair, a chess set, an open sewing basket and a log fire crackling in the grate. At the other was a rustic kitchen. A kettle whistled on the stove next to an iron pot of simmering rabbit stew. Candles flickered on the thick chunk of roughly sculpted wood that passed for a table. It was littered with scrunched-up plans and diagrams of toys, half-built matchstick models, knitting, piles of letters, packets of biscuits, six iron horseshoes and a photograph of a white-haired couple and a cheeky young man with a mischievous grin.

The snow leopard padded through the room and climbed a circular flight of stairs, partially hidden behind a lopsided dresser. Pinned to the side of the dresser was a list of things to do:

~~write list of things to do~~

plan route

check loading

check Present Ledger

invent new toys

fit magic reindeer shoes

Upstairs there were two small bedrooms. One was presently unoccupied. The other was the scene of an argument.

"Bother!" boomed a man's voice. "It's too tight!"

"Of course it's too tight, you old fool," replied a woman's voice. "Your stomach has grown!"

The snow leopard pushed his way into the room and made himself comfortable on the bed next to the woman. She was a stout old lady with a mouthful of pins and a shock of white hair. Standing directly in front of her was her husband, who was even stouter. He had a belly as big as a beer barrel and a bushy white beard that he'd swept over his shoulder like a scarf.

"Well, it fitted me last year!" he grumbled. He was wearing a moth-eaten pair of red woollen trousers and a red fur-lined coat with a row of gold buttons down the front. Only there weren't any buttons on the coat, because they'd all popped off, and the woman was trying to sew them back on again.

"Theo! Stand still!" she cried as he turned away to stick another yellow Post-it note on the wall and her thread snapped. The button rolled under the bed and Mrs Christmas bent down to retrieve it. "I don't know why you don't just get the elves to make you a new costume!" she said crossly.

"Because this is the original one, Gertie. It's part of the tradition. Where would the world be if Father Christmas did his rounds in a leopard-skin leotard?"

At the mention of "leopard skin" the snow leopard dived under a pillow and hid.

"Not *your* skin, Custard. Look at him. Call yourself a snow leopard!" He chuckled. "You're just a great big scaredy-cat!"

The button clattered to the floor again and Mrs Christmas growled.

Mr Christmas was not making it easy for his wife. While she was trying to repair his red coat, he was trying to plan his route for Christmas Eve. He had a list of every name of every child in the world and an *A–Z of the Skies*. He was writing every child's name down on a yellow Post-it note, then sticking the notes to the furniture and walls in alphabetical order. The room was covered in yellow notes from ceiling to floor.

"Oh, by the way," he yelped excitedly, "did I tell you about my new invention?"

"Not yet," sighed his wife wearily.

Mr Christmas leant across to the bedside table and pulled a strange-looking object out of a drawer.

It was a misshapen ball, its roundness stretched out of shape by a triangular object inside, a bit like a small child's mouth with a long shortbread finger jammed in widthways.

"It's a ball that always comes back," he said. "It's got a boomerang inside."

"It looks more like a coat hanger," Mrs Christmas replied.

"Well, yes…" Her husband blushed. "It *is* a coat hanger, actually. Do you think there's time to get it into stockings for this year?"

"No," said Mrs Christmas firmly. "It's Christmas Eve. The elves have got enough to do without making a billion new toys for you." But she might as well have been talking to herself, because Mr Christmas was thinking up a name for his new invention.

"Hmm," he mused. "Boomall or ballerang?" He absent-mindedly tossed the toy to one side expecting it to return to his hand, but Mr Christmas's inventions had a habit of not working first time. The boomall/ballerang ricocheted round the room, shaved Gertie's glasses, whacked Custard on the nose and crashed through the window.

"Bother!" said Mr Christmas as the last shard of glass tinkled into the courtyard below.

"All done!" announced Mrs Christmas. She snapped the thread off the final button and stood up. "Now turn round, Theo, and see what you think."

Mr Christmas put his hands in his pockets, puffed out his chest and admired his figure in the mirror.

11

Unfortunately his stomach was too big and the suit too small for the stretch. One by one the buttons shot off across the floor.

"Bother!" he exclaimed.

"You are going on a diet," Mrs Christmas said crossly, but Mr Christmas wasn't listening. He had found a walnut in his pocket.

"Would you believe it!" he cried. "I made this for Mudrick last year and forgot to give it to him." He split the walnut in half and showed his wife the miniature hand-carved chess set inside.

"You spoil that boy," she said.

"What's wrong with giving him presents?" he replied. "He's our son."

"Who never writes and who only phones when he needs money," she snapped.

Mr Christmas shook his head and stuck another Post-it note on the wall. "He's changed, Gertie. When I found him on the streets he was wild, yes. But now, he's at business college, he's passed exams – why, he's probably even bagged himself a filly!"

"Don't be rude," she said, turning her back on him so he couldn't see her smile. Mr Christmas kissed her, but she shook him off and pretended not to like it.

"You were my filly once!" he said.

"That's enough, Theo. I only hope college has made him less selfish."

"Well, we'll find out in a few hours, won't we?" he said as he pinned another note on the wall. "There! Finished! Sky route planned!" Then he

12

pointed to the sea of yellow Post-its and said, "First stop: Aaron Aardvark, Australia. Second stop: Aaron Aaronovitch, Poland. Third stop: Aaron Abergwhenny, Wales."

Mrs Christmas shook her head wearily. "So you'll have travelled once round the world and only delivered three presents," she said for the umpteenth time. "Why not do one country at a time?"

"Because alphabetical's the only way to make sure every child gets their present," he declared.

"You're the boss," she sighed, in a way that made Mr Christmas feel extremely unbosslike. He checked the present list again in case he'd made a mistake, and discovered to his horror that he had.

"Bother! I've missed out Abelard Affleck!"

Mrs Christmas did *not* smile triumphantly, when it would have been easy to do so. Instead, she gathered up her sewing basket and left the room, while her husband tore the yellow Post-it notes off the wall, crumpled them up and chucked them out of the window.

"Now I'm going to have to start again!" he yelled. "Bother! Bother! Bother! Bother! Bother!"

CHAPTER TWO

It just so happened that passing underneath the window at that moment was an elf called Tobin. Tobin was in charge of the toy factory, a weighty responsibility reflected in the number of worry lines on his forehead. He was muttering darkly to himself when the Post-it notes hit him in the face.

"Oh, yes, check the stinking reindeer as well, Tobin! And while you're at it, run the factory, wrap the presents and load the sleigh! Oh, and Tobin, I need six pints of blood. Roll up your sleeve. Ow!"

He was not having a good day. And it didn't get any better when the youngest of the magic reindeer, an earnest chap called Dasher, cantered up to ask him a question.

"Mr Tobin—"

"What are you doing out here?" cried the stressed elf. "You're supposed to be putting your magic shoes on."

"Might I have a word?" asked Dasher.

"I'll give you a word," said Tobin dryly. "Over-worked."

"No," said the reindeer, missing the joke. "I want to speak to you. I've lost a tooth. I need your help."

But Tobin was a busy man. He turned suddenly and disappeared into the stables. Unfortunately Dasher was watching Tobin and not where he was going. As Tobin walked through the door, Dasher turned head first into the stable wall and knocked himself out.

Tobin was expecting to find the reindeer shod and groomed for the big present pull that night. What he found came as a nasty shock. Not one reindeer was close to being ready. There was a card game in progress at the back of the stables. Blitzen, Vixen, Dancer and Donner were playing poker for grass stakes, while down at the front, Comet, a flighty-headed female, was pinning heated rollers into Prancer's hair. Prancer was prone to hysterics and had refused to fly without a perm.

"What is going on in here?" gasped Tobin. "Don't reindeer ever take responsibility for themselves?"

"I'm responsible for the poker game!" Blitzen guffawed.

"Where's Pots?"

Pots was the simple-minded elf whose job it was to look after the reindeer, but a basic lack of common sense and an unfortunate case of sticky-out ears had turned him into a figure of fun.

15

"Pots went to find Mr Christmas," said Prancer, fluffing his curls with a hoof.

"And Rudolph?" said Tobin. "Where's he?"

"He went to find Pots." Comet giggled.

"And failed!" boomed Captain Rudolph as he marched through the stable door.

Rudolph was the most honest and decent reindeer you could wish to meet. He trusted people to do what they promised and when they let him down he was always surprised.

"Pots has gone AWOL again. Can't find him anywhere! At this rate we'll never get shod—" He stopped in mid-sentence and peered at a scattering of grass by the door. "What's happened to the extra grass rations?" he exclaimed. "That was the pre-flight vitamin supplement!"

"We ate it," sniggered Donner, showing off a mouth full of green teeth.

"But we're taking off in T minus ten hours!" shouted Rudolph.

"Not unless we've got shoes on, we're not!" Vixen yawned, sliding out of the shadows. "And just for the record, if I'm made lead reindeer this year I'm not going. Someone else can do all the hard work. I want a nice cushy ride at the back."

"Hear, hear!" cried Blitzen, a fellow trouble-maker.

"But you two *always* go at the back," said Rudolph sourly.

"And me!" squeaked Prancer, tossing his curls around his antlers. "I'm not going at the front either.

16

Last time I did, I trod on the Dog Star. It bit my hoof!"

Tobin gave up. He did not have time for bickering reindeer. "What upsets me most," he said to Rudolph as he turned to leave, "is that the boss thinks Christmas happens all by itself!"

Rudolph raised an eyebrow. "Where's your Christmas spirit?" he asked.

"I drank it," said the overworked elf. "To numb the pain."

Most people found Mr Christmas's bumbling, old-fashioned ways quite charming. It would be fair to say that Tobin was not amongst them.

Nor was the formidable Sealeater, the organizer of the packers and stackers. In the middle of the night, Papagrolin, the senior elf, whose wisdom had calmed many a stormy sea, had asked her to recheck the present for Jamila Nicely.

"I am not unpacking and repacking that sleigh again!" she shrieked. "I've only just finished re-repacking it because of Baz Hogan's surfboard. Mr C said we'd packed a skateboard by mistake!"

"And what had you packed?" asked the old elf patiently.

"Well, a skateboard," growled Sealeater, "but that's not the point."

Papagrolin held up a miniature spice rack. "So what's going to happen on Christmas morning when Jamila opens her tropical barbecue and finds that the spice rack's missing?" he said.

"Oh ... give it here," she snapped, snatching the

spice rack out of Papagrolin's hand and blowing sharply on a whistle. She was cross with herself for giving in so quickly, even though she knew it was the right thing to do.

"UNPACKING AGAIN, GIRLS!" she bellowed.

Her assistants groaned at the prospect of unpacking more than three billion presents for the forty-third time.

Tank was another elf with a grievance. He was big, with a huge, muscly frame that required feeding every twenty minutes. Earlier that morning he too had been bending Papagrolin's ear.

"I ain't got time to weave each of these hobbyhorses a different coloured tail!" he said. "An elf's got to eat, you know!"

"Tank, you know Mr Christmas's rules," said Papagrolin. "Every present must be made to fit the child."

"Well, blow Mr Christmas's rules," shouted Tank. "I'm not happy. And I'm hungry too."

"You're always hungry," said the older elf as Tank's mobile phone rang.

"No!" panicked Papagrolin. "Put it away. You know Mr Christmas hates newfangled gadgets!"

But Tank paid no attention. He answered the phone, grunted, then rang off.

"Great!" he growled. "Now my supper's burnt!"

"Bit early for supper, isn't it?" remarked Papagrolin.

"Last Friday's supper," hissed Tank. "I haven't been home for six days!"

18

"Well, you'll get home tomorrow," said Papa-grolin, "guaranteed. The trick is not to think of the work – think of the *joy* your work is going to bring to all those little children."

"Poppycock!" roared Tank. "My back is killing me!"

Mr Christmas knew nothing about it, but there was mutiny in the air.

CHAPTER THREE

Mr Christmas stepped out of the cottage with six safety pins holding his red jacket together. He stopped on the doorstep and sucked in a deep breath of cold air.

"Aaaah!" he gasped. "Delicious! There'll be fresh snow tonight." Then he bent down, picked up his boomall/ballerang and slotted it into his black belt.

"Mr Christmas!"

He recognized the voice immediately. It was Tobin, and Tobin generally didn't call out unless there was trouble, and if there *was* trouble Mr Christmas would rather be a million miles away. He turned and walked in the opposite direction, pretending that he hadn't heard the call, but Tobin caught up with him and tapped him on the shoulder.

"Mr Christmas!"

"Ah, Tobin!" The old man beamed, trying to hide his attempt to escape with a fulsome greeting. He rather overdid it, clasping Tobin to his chest and squeezing him until the elf was gasping for breath. "What a pleasure to see you. How are you?"

"Tired," said Tobin.

"Oh dear," said Mr Christmas. "More staff problems?" Staff problems had always baffled Mr Christmas. He loved every minute of his work and assumed that everyone else did too. "It's not pep-talk time again, is it?"

Tobin nodded. "I'm afraid so. The reindeer are shoeless, Tank is hungry, and the packers and stackers are revolting."

"Bother!" said Mr Christmas, because bother it was.

With Tobin by his side, Mr Christmas reluctantly set off for the factory, only to find his path blocked by three lacklustre reindeer.

"Is this a good time to discuss the purchase of a television for the reindeer's waiting room?" asked Vixen.

"Only last time we asked, you said we should ask again later," Blitzen added.

The old man's face drained of colour until it was whiter than his beard.

"No! No! No! No! No!" he howled. "No to television! It rots the brain. Turns freethinkers into walking vegetables. It sucks out invention. There's nothing good there. Just half-baked programmes stuffing your head with pap and nonsense! Learn the piano instead." And he stomped off, leaving the reindeer looking glum.

21

"I can tell you've never tinkled the ivories with hooves," Prancer muttered after him. "'Flight of the Bumble Bee' is a bit tricky, I can tell you."

The factory floor was chaotic. Hundreds of elves were busy doing hundreds of different jobs, and the steamy air was thick with curses and cries and the never-ending background noise of whistles and clanks and rattles and booms. Pistons crashed, lathes screamed, conveyor belts rumbled and boxes of toys trundled along metal rollers to the far end of the barn, where they were labelled then passed out to Sealeater to be wrapped and loaded onto the magic sleigh.

Mr Christmas entered the factory with Tobin. He climbed on top of a box so that he could be seen and waved his beard in the air to attract the elves' attention. When the noise had died down he began his pep talk.

"Morning," he said.

"Morning, Mr Christmas," replied the lone voice of Papagrolin, who was the only elf to greet his boss with a smile.

"I do wish you'd call me Theo," said Mr Christmas. "Morning, Tank, how are the hobby-horses? Tails blue, tails green, tails as bright as a rainbow seen?"

Tank was too hungry to talk. Instead he snapped the head off the hobby-horse in his hand. Mr Christmas looked confused.

"I think that means 'coming along fine'," lied Papagrolin.

"Oh good!" said the old man. "I just wanted to say happy Christmas Eve to you all, and from all the children in the world a great big thank you!" He turned to Tobin and sought his approval. "There," he said. "Peppy enough for you?"

"It'll have to do," sighed Tobin.

"What are you moping about?" said Mr Christmas. "You know I couldn't do Christmas without you."

Tobin checked that he had the support of the factory floor before starting what was going to be an awkward speech.

"Er ... since you're asking," he said nervously, "we all feel—"

But before he could say another word, he was interrupted by a shrill "Whoop!" Mr Christmas had suddenly remembered the new toy in his belt.

"Oh bother! Sorry. Mind like a grasshopper! Clean forgot." He held up the boomall/ballerang for everyone to see. "Must just ask you. This new toy. Don't spare my feelings. What do you think?"

"What is it?" asked Tank.

"I'll show you," said Mr Christmas, and he bounced the strangely shaped object on the floor, whereupon it shot off at an unexpected angle and criss-crossed the factory like a bullet. The elves screamed and hurled themselves under their machines for protection, but Tank was too big to crawl under his machine and the boomall/ ballerang struck him right between the eyes with a dead *thwack*.

"It's a ball that comes back," said Mr Christmas.

"Not any more, it isn't!" growled Tank, peeling the boomall/ballerang off his forehead and bouncing it through the glass window. Outside, a startled Custard screeched. Then there was silence.

Eventually Tobin spoke.

"It's not that we don't like your ideas, Mr Christmas, it's just that we feel we could be more efficient. Every year you want us to make more and more toys on machines that were built before the Ark."

Mr Christmas chuckled out loud. "What a flood that was, eh, Tobin! Got our feet wet in the Gobi Desert."

"Yes, but the point is, you want all of these toys made to higher and higher standards."

"Well, we don't want them to break, do we?"

"Something's got to give," explained the elf wearily.

"Oh! You want me to give you something!" said Mr Christmas cheerfully. "What would you like? A pet rabbit, a drinks cabinet, golfing socks?"

"I'd like," said Tobin, "to modernize our systems…"

But his words were drowned out by the loud whine of a klaxon and a voice shouting, "Husky Bus coming in!"

"Everybody out!" cried a joyful Mr Christmas, rushing for the door. "Mudrick's here!"

"Oh, sound the trumpets!" muttered Tobin peevishly. "The prodigal son hath returned."

CHAPTER FOUR

As Mr Christmas ran to greet his son, a wet nose nudged him in the back and sent him sprawling across the snow.

"Sorry," said Dasher. "I only wanted to catch your attention."

"Well, you've certainly done that," said Mr Christmas, pulling off his boots and shaking out the snow that was packed around his socks.

Dasher took a deep breath to stop himself from crying. "Mr Christmas, I've lost a tooth!" he said.

"Then I hope you find it," replied the old man. "Now, if that's all, Dasher, I really must get along."

The young reindeer looked forlorn, but Mr Christmas had already marched across the snow-covered courtyard and helped himself to Papagrolin's telescope.

"Let the dog see the rabbit!" he said to the senior elf, putting the telescope to his eye and following his son's progress across the snowfields.

Mudrick was riding the Husky Bus from Reykjavik, an extra-large sleigh with on-board toilets and a coffee machine. He was lying across the back seats covered in a sheepskin rug, playing with a hand-held computer game. He was looking healthy, Mr Christmas thought. Not bad for a student. His clothes were scruffier than Mrs Christmas would have liked, but his face was as mischievous and alive as ever – that trademark black quiff, that snaggled-toothed gap in his smile and those freckles!

Mrs Christmas ran out of the cottage wearing an apron covered in white floury fingerprints, waving a large handkerchief in case she was overcome with emotion.

"Mudrick!" she called as the Husky Bus drew up in the courtyard. "Yoo-hoo! Mudrick!"

He was thumping the computer game in his lap and muttering "Useless junk!" when she slid alongside him and threw out her arms for a hug.

"Cheers!" he said, stepping out of the Husky Bus and hanging his rucksack over her outstretched arms. "Wow! Look at that!" He'd caught sight of the magic sleigh laden with Father Christmas's presents. It was an impressive sight. "What a fat load of presents, man!" And, ignoring his poor mother-cum-hatstand, he sprinted over to the sleigh and ran his hands greedily over the parcels. "I dream of having your job, Dad. If you could *sell* all these presents, you'd be well wonged up!"

"How are you, Mudrick?" said Mr Christmas, who had followed his son across the courtyard.

"Skint," said the boy. "Spent my last thirty crowns on this heap of tat." He thrust his computer game in his father's face. "Calls itself Goblin Wars, but have I seen Gandor the Goblin King? Have I squat! And as for raising a goblin army, all I've collected so far are six sheep and a wine bladder. It's useless!" And, so saying, he chucked it away into the snow, narrowly missing his mother, who was trotting across to greet her son for a second time.

Mrs Christmas was not going to lose her temper with Mudrick so early on in the holiday. "Haven't you got a kiss for your old mum?" she asked cheerily.

"In a minute," said Mudrick, putting his arm round his father's shoulder and deliberately leading him away from his mother. "You see, I've been thinking," he whispered conspiratorially. "One day this is all going to be mine, right? So can I have it now?"

Mr Christmas laughed at such a preposterous idea.

"No, I'm serious," said Mudrick. "College has taught me to think big, right. So I'm thinking millionaire before I'm twenty! But to do it I'm going to need all the cash I can squeeze out of the family business."

Mr Christmas's heart sank. "This isn't a family business," he said. "You can't inherit Father Christmas."

"So why did you adopt me then?" Mudrick asked.

Mr Christmas was stunned by the bluntness of the question. "Er … because we love you."

"No." Mudrick grinned. "No! I don't believe you. Really?"

There was an awkward silence. The embarrassed elves shuffled their feet in the snow as Mrs Christmas retraced her steps into the kitchen and the front door clicked shut.

Mudrick felt guilty. He should have said hello. He abandoned his father and ran towards the cottage, but halfway across the courtyard Dasher stepped into his path.

"I wouldn't normally ask," trembled the reindeer, "but you're the only one who can help me! You've been out in the other world, Mr Mudrick. You know about things."

"What things?" said the boy. "What do you want?"

"I lost my tooth last night. Put it under my pillow and it was still there this morning. The Tooth Fairy never came."

"Did you send an email?" asked Mudrick.

"Email?" repeated Dasher.

"You stick-headed creature!" mocked the boy. "Don't you watch the news?"

"How can he?" shouted a voice from inside the stables. "Telly is banned! Like everything else in this prison."

"That's quite enough, thank you, Vixen!" shouted

Rudolph, who was no fan of sarcasm. "If I want to hear your cheerful voice again I'll ask for it."

"The Tooth Fairy's gone virtual," Mudrick told Dasher.

"What's that?" asked the young reindeer.

Mudrick patted him on the head. "It's a bit like your brain," he said patronizingly. "It doesn't exist!"

Five minutes later, while Mrs Christmas made lobster sandwiches for Mr Christmas's in-flight dinner, Mudrick confronted his mother.

"Is that really why you adopted me?" he asked. "Because you *love* me?"

"Of course," she said.

"You didn't bring me in to join the firm? You know, Father Christmas *and Son*? I just assumed that one day I'd be taking over."

"No need," she said. "Your father is immortal."

"But don't you think a change would be for the best?" pressed Mudrick.

"No," she said. "If Father Christmas changes, the magic dies." There! Now Mudrick knew. And that, she thought, was that.

Suddenly the room grew darker. The air filled with clouds of black smoke that settled on the freshly cut sandwiches, and from the chimney came a terrifying clatter.

"Aaaagh! Hooooo! Whooop! Yaaaah!"

A young elf with goofy teeth and ears like jug handles tumbled out of the chimney and rolled

29

across the floor. He jumped up in a storm of soot clouds. His hair stuck out wildly, and pasted across his smutty face was a great big gormless grin.

"Sorry, Mrs Christmas," he chirped.

"Hello, Pots," she said, casting a generous smile in the hapless elf's direction. "You see, Mudrick, some things are never meant to change."

"Hello, Mr Mudrick," said the elf, but the graceless youth did not reply. He had already picked up his rucksack and disappeared upstairs.

Pots was a simple-minded innocent who loved everyone regardless of how they treated him, and who was loyal even to those who took advantage of his good nature. If, as a joke, Mudrick had asked him to run to the four corners of the earth, Pots would willingly have done it. He only wanted to please.

"What am I doing here?" he asked.

"I don't know, Pots," she said. "But Mr Christmas has been looking for you."

"Mr Christmas has been looking for me? But I've been looking for Mr Christmas."

"We know. He's here now."

Pots whipped his eyes round the room like a nervous gunfighter expecting an ambush from all sides at once.

"Here? Now? Where? Is he invisible?"

Mrs Christmas laid a calming hand on his shoulder. "Pots," she said. "How can I help you?"

For no apparent reason Pots suddenly burst into tears. "Oh, Mrs Christmas, I want you to know that

I *love* the reindeer. They are my life. If they were ever to go in the mincer for dog food I think I would die."

"I know, Pots," she said sympathetically. "Now don't upset yourself."

"Don't upset myself?" snuffled the elf, wiping away the tears. "But I *can't* help upsetting myself, Mrs Christmas. I can't get rid of the pictures in my head … their magic hooves in the mincer!"

"Try," she said. Then in order to bring the conversation swiftly to the point, she added, "What did you want to see Mr Christmas about?"

"I don't know," gasped Pots.

"Is it about that letter in your hand?"

"No," he said. "Yes. It is! A man gave this letter to me."

"Good," said Mrs Christmas, taking the letter and laying it down on the table. "Mr Christmas can read it when he gets back."

At that precise moment, Mr Christmas was trying to reach the sleigh hut to triple-check the packed presents, but an upset reindeer wouldn't let him pass. Dasher had shut the doors to the hut and had chained himself to the handles like a suffragette. He wasn't budging until Mr Christmas had answered his question.

"Mudrick said that the Tooth Fairy's gone virtual," he sobbed. "Does that means she's dead?"

Mr Christmas shook his head. "No, Dasher. I think it means she's lost her magic."

"So there won't be any money?"

"Only for the man who owns her," said Mr Christmas.

He was right. The Tooth Fairy had been bought by Mike Mammon, a greedy businessman who had only one ambition – to get rich, to stay rich and to get even richer while doing it. He had turned the Tooth Fairy into teethintocash.com, an Internet company that promised to "Put money where your mouth is!" It was just a scam to extract cash (and teeth) from children and their soft parents, who *paid* teethintocash.com to take their children's milk teeth away. The children received one pound per tooth, but only *after* their parents had paid five pounds for a genuine teethintocash.com milk tooth diploma. And that wasn't all. Teethintocash.com was now offering bonuses to children if they pulled their teeth out before they fell out naturally! The reason? So that teethintocash.com could sell them to a denture manufacturer and make a tidy extra profit out of falsies for old-age elves!

Having unpacked his bag, Mudrick came back downstairs to the kitchen. He stared at Pots with undisguised contempt. Pots grinned back.

"Shouldn't you be getting the reindeer ready for tonight?" said Mrs Christmas, steering Pots towards the door before Mudrick could say something nasty.

"I should be getting the reindeer ready for tonight, yes," said Pots. "How do I do that then, Mrs Christmas?"

"Put on their magic shoes," she said.

"Oh yes, of course," said Pots, backing out of the door. "Put on their magic shoes. Put on their magic shoes. Put on their magic shoes. Put on their magic shoes!" His muttering continued until he was well inside the stables.

Meanwhile Mudrick had picked up the letter off the table.

"I don't know why you put up with that straw-brain!" he sneered.

His mother sighed. Mudrick had never been kind. "Take that letter to your father," she said, "while I fill his flask. And NO reading!"

Mudrick turned in the doorway, apparently offended that she should need to tell him.

"As if I would," he said with a mocking smile.

As he was making his way across the courtyard to deal with the magic reindeer shoes, Pots found a hand-held computer game buried in the snow. He was astonished that anyone would throw away something so new. He picked it up and popped it in his pocket before anyone noticed.

A minute or so later, Mudrick emerged from the cottage with his father's letter in his hand. He had of course opened it and was now riveted by its contents.

19 DECEMBER

DEAR MR CHRISTMAS,

YOU MUST KNOW ME. I'M FAMOUS! LAST YEAR I BOUGHT THE TOOTH FAIRY AND TURNED HER INTO A HIGHLY PROFITABLE DOTCOM COMPANY CALLED <u>TEETHINTOCASH.COM</u>. I HAVE JUST DONE THE SAME WITH EASTER. <u>BUNNYMONEY.COM</u> WILL SOON BE THE ONLY PLACE ON THE PLANET TO BUY CHOCOLATE EASTER EGGS. WHEN WE GO ONLINE I EXPECT TO BECOME THE RICHEST MAN IN THE WORLD.

TO THE POINT. WHILE LOOKING AROUND FOR NEW ACQUISITIONS I CAME ACROSS YOUR NAME IN THE PHONE BOOK. HOW ABOUT IT? WILL YOU SELL ME FATHER CHRISTMAS? LOADS OF DOSH FOR BOTH OF US WHEN YOU DO. GET BACK SOONEST.

YOURS WITH TONGUE HANGING OUT IN ANTICI-PATION OF JOINT MEMBERSHIP OF BILLIONAIRE CLUB!

MIKE MAMMON

When Mudrick lowered the piece of paper his eyes were sticking out on stalks.

CHAPTER FIVE

Mudrick found his father in the dark green sleigh hut, surrounded by an agitated Sealeater, an irritated Tobin and a supportive Papagrolin. That is to say, Papagrolin was supporting a huge ledger on his back, in which over three billion names had painstakingly been written by hand. This was the Present Ledger. Every child in the world appeared in this ledger with the toy of their choice inscribed opposite their name. There were five columns to the right of the present entries. There was a column for when the toy was made, a column for when it was loaded onto the sleigh, a column for when it was first checked, a column for when it was double-checked and a column for when it was triple-checked. The first four columns had been filled in. Mr Christmas was filling in the fifth as he checked the double-checks again. With four thousand eight hundred and twenty-five pages to examine, it was taking a fair bit of time.

"Courage, Papagrolin!" exhorted Mr Christmas as the faithful old elf groaned under the weight of the ledger. "Only sixty million entries left to check!"

"You're not still using *that* old thing, are you?" sneered Mudrick. "A computer would be much faster, Dad. You could transfer the data in a couple of hours and—"

Mr Christmas did not look up from his task, but the firmness of his reply left Mudrick in no doubt as to where he stood on computers.

"Never! Computers break down! Computers crash and burn! And when they do, Mudrick, all those little letters that are stored in their electronic brains just disappear. Files, folders, whole pages of words and sentences simply melt away. But pen and paper stays put. I can see what I've written. I can touch it. I can trust it. Aha! Look!" There was a hint of triumph in his voice. "Emerson Trudeau, Canada. Did we remake the tin soldiers *without* guns, according to his mother's specifications?"

Tobin shook his head.

"Then we must change it!"

"But, Mr C," pleaded Sealeater, "it's all been checked and double-checked. Don't make us do it again!"

"Sorry, old friend," he said. "But if one child gets the wrong toy then we've failed."

"Dad," said Mudrick, producing the letter from Mike Mammon, "can I have a quick word?"

"Oh bother!" exploded Mr Christmas suddenly,

leaping into the air as if stung by a hornet. "The reindeer's shoes!" And he ran outside without so much as a backward glance.

Only after Mr Christmas had left did Papagrolin sink to his knees.

"Someone take this book off me!" he cried.

Sealeater obliged, while Tobin whispered treachery into Mudrick's ear.

"Sometimes," he said, "I don't think your father's got both hands on the reins."

"Then it's up to us to take the reins off him!" said the boy, waving the letter under Tobin's nose and giving the elf a sly wink.

Mr Christmas was horrified to find that most of the reindeer were still asleep. Rudolph and Dasher were the only ones awake. Both were polishing their bridles.

"Bother, bother, bother!" cried Mr Christmas. "Still no Pots?"

"No, sir. But he's back," said Rudolph.

"Then why have none of you got shoes on?"

"You'll have to ask him that, sir," said Rudolph, pointing to the forge out the back from where a strange clanking noise was coming.

When Pots appeared he was over ten feet tall and was swaying from side to side like a circus stilt walker.

Mr Christmas exploded with laughter. "Dear me, Pots! What on earth have you done to yourself?"

"I have put on the magic shoes just like Mrs

Christmas told me to," he said.

"On the *reindeer*!" roared Mr Christmas. Pots had nailed sixteen magic reindeer shoes to the bottom of each boot. "You stupid boy!"

While a crestfallen Pots prised off the iron shoes, Mr Christmas roused the lazy reindeer by blowing a bugle. They woke with a start, not knowing where they were or what was happening.

"Take-off in ten minutes!" he shouted as Mudrick crept up behind him and tugged his arm.

"Can I have a word *now*?" he asked.

"Later," said his father, raising his voice to rally the troops. "Right. Who wants to go at the front this year? Let's see a show of hooves."

The reindeer stared at Mr Christmas as if he was mad. Nobody raised a hoof, so he made the choice for them.

"Rudolph and Dasher, will you take the lead again?"

"Pleasure's all ours, sir!" said the two reindeer, but it wasn't really a pleasure at all. They'd been front-runners for the last fifteen years. It was extremely hard work and secretly they had hoped that this year one of the others might volunteer.

"Good lads!" Mr Christmas beamed, rubbing Dasher's antlers. "Shoes on, team! I'll be back!"

Mr Christmas rushed into the kitchen, grabbed his scarf and hat off the hook on the back of the door and pointed to the wooden cuckoo clock.

"Six o'clock, Gertie. Ready to go."

On the table Mrs Christmas had laid out her husband's packed supper. Apple spice cake, cinnamon buns, lobster sandwiches, gingerbread biscuits, a flask of hot tea and three bottles of Old Socks Beer.

"Oh, rumble-o my tumble-o!" he drooled, wiping the spit off his chin with his beard. His greedy fingers edged towards the cake, but Mrs Christmas slapped them away with a fish slice.

"Dad, please!" said Mudrick, rushing into the kitchen and stepping between his father and the feast. "Before you go, you must read this letter."

"No time, Mudrick. The world awaits!"

"But it's from Mike Mammon. He wants to buy Father Christmas."

"What?" said Mr Christmas. You could have heard a pin drop.

Mudrick held out the letter, which his father took, unfolded and read.

"I thought I told you not to open that letter!" Mrs Christmas said sharply to her son.

"Er … I didn't," lied Mudrick unconvincingly. "It accidentally fluttered onto a reindeer's antler and split open."

"Ha!" There was an explosion of contempt from the old man in red. He screwed up the letter and threw it over his shoulder. "Not for sale!" he declared, dragging the heavy picnic basket off the table. "Father Christmas belongs to everyone. He's not mine to give away." Then he gave his wife a goodbye kiss and headed for the door.

"But you're not giving anything away," argued Mudrick. "He wants to buy it. This could make you rich."

Mr Christmas stopped in the doorway. From the stillness of his shoulders it was clear that he was angry.

"I'm in a hurry, Mudrick."

"OK. OK!" Mudrick was thinking on his feet. "So why don't we just steal his idea? Set up fatherchristmas.com ourselves, sell presents online and clean up!"

"Because," said Mr Christmas, turning to face his son and speaking slowly to make himself clear, "*I don't make profits!* Now, if you'll excuse me, I've got three billion forty million seven hundred and thirty-two thousand five hundred and ninety-three presents to deliver. Goodnight." And he left the kitchen.

CHAPTER SIX

When Mr Christmas stepped outside it was snowing. He smiled as he remembered his prediction. "Never wrong," he said to himself. "Never wrong."

The sleigh was standing in the middle of the courtyard covered in a sparkling white coat of snow. In the back sat Tobin, the navigator. He was huddled in a blanket, sulking. He hated flying. The reindeer stood harnessed in two rows of four. At the front Rudolph and Dasher held their heads high in readiness for the off, but at the back Blitzen and Vixen slouched against the sleigh, grumbling.

"You tell him."

"*You* tell him."

"I told him last time."

"You did not."

"I did."

"Silence in the ranks!" bellowed Rudolph.

There was a brief lull in the bickering, then

Prancer leant towards Vixen and whispered, "Tell him what?"

"That we're fed up of delivering presents alphabetically and flying round the world millions of times more than we need to," she said.

"You are so right," said Prancer. "You *should* tell him."

"Tell him *what*?" roared Rudolph.

"That it would be less tiring if we just flew around the world *once*!" said Donner.

Rudolph unclipped himself from his harness and walked briskly down the line like a sergeant major.

"Well, I've got a little surprise for you lot. You are *magic* reindeer. It is your job to pull Father Christmas's magic sleigh, and if he says jump through fire you jump through fire! Is that understood? And if you don't like it, you can go and haul firewood through the wolf packs of the Arctic tundra! Am I making myself clear?"

"As mud," muttered Vixen as Mr Christmas eased himself into the sleigh.

"Tobin!" he shouted. "Ready to see the world?"

"Can't someone else navigate for once?" said his reluctant passenger. "I get air sick."

"I know," said Mr Christmas sympathetically. "Poor Tobin." Then with a roaring laugh he tossed something to the bilious elf. "That's why I brought the sick bags!" Turning to Pots he cried, "Fire up the talismanic motor!"

Pots stepped forward, took hold of the rope

underneath Mr Christmas's seat and gave it a sharp tug as if he was starting a lawnmower. The motor had been in storage for a year, and backfired several times before finally stuttering into life. Custard thought it was a hunter firing a gun and jumped into Mrs Christmas's arms. As it picked up anti-gravitational thrust the talismanic motor started to hum and spread a warm purple glow across the snow.

"Tally-ho, boys, tally-ho!" cried Mr Christmas as he flicked the reins, and Rudolph and Dasher put their new magic shoes to the test.

The sleigh glided out of the courtyard into a nearby field, where it took off. Mrs Christmas and Custard waved goodbye until it was no more than a tiny black dot in the sky. Then Mrs Christmas turned back towards the cottage, wiping away a tear.

"I'm like this with bagpipes too," she sniffed, kissing the snow leopard on his head. "Oh, Custard." She smiled. "I do love Christmas!" Then she filled her lungs and let out a roar that terrified the whales in Newfoundland. "Mudrick! I want several words with you!"

Later that night, on an ice floe at the South Pole, a family of emperor penguins stood in a line and watched the magic sleigh pass overhead. They watched and watched, and leant back and watched. Then one of them tumbled backwards, and they all fell, knocking each other down like a row of

43

CHAPTER SEVEN

Despite the difficulties of getting airborne with the right presents on board, the present run went remarkably smoothly. Admittedly the magic sleigh had to circumnavigate the world billions of times due to Mr Christmas's eccentric mapping system, but every child got the right present, and every mince pie, carrot and bottle of beer left out for Father Christmas and the reindeer was collected and stowed on board.

There was one nasty moment over a motorway just outside Tokyo, when Mr Christmas flew too low and flashed through a speed camera at sixty-two thousand miles per hour. A waiting police car switched on its flashing light and gave chase, but it was no match for the magic sleigh and Mr Christmas escaped. When they developed the film in the speed camera and saw who they had caught, the police decided not to prosecute. It was Christmas, after all, the season of goodwill and all that. Instead they asked Mr Christmas if they could use the photograph as their Christmas card next year, and Mr Christmas said yes.

Custard was out chasing an Arctic fox when the sleigh returned home. Its long moonshadow fell across his path and frightened him half to death. He thought he was being chased by a flying polar bear.

When the sleigh came to a standstill there was a moment's silence while the reindeer caught their breath, and an ashen-faced Tobin lurched out into the snow clutching a white paper bag.

"I think I've just been sick on every capital city in the world," he groaned.

"Well done, team!" croaked Mr Christmas. "Mission accomplished!" He looked tired but elated as he opened the sleigh door. Before he could stand up, however, a landslide of carrots and mince pies pushed him out of the sleigh and buried him up to his waist.

The sight of so many carrots turned the reindeer's stomachs. Comet and Dasher quelled their nausea by pressing cold snow-compresses onto each other's temples.

"I couldn't eat another carrot if you paid me," whimpered Comet, clutching her stomach and belching like a bullfrog.

Mr Christmas was still carrot-bound a minute or so later when a blanket was thrown across his shoulders and a steaming hot mug of chocolate was thrust into his hands.

"Dad! Hi! Welcome back," said Mudrick. "Don't move while I dig you out. You must be exhausted. Drink up."

Mr Christmas took a swig and coughed.

"It's got rum in it," said the boy, "as a pick-me-up!" He helped his father to his feet and gently walked him to the cottage. "I've run you a bath and put a hot-water bottle in your bed."

"No, Mudrick, stop!" said Mr Christmas, easing his son off his shoulder and turning round to face him. "I can't just go to bed. There are things to do. The sleigh to put away, the reindeer—"

"Dad! Leave everything to me." Mudrick smiled, turning his father round again and pushing him gently homeward. "You need to get some rest. It's all taken care of."

"You're not ill, are you, Mudrick?" asked Mr Christmas.

"No," said his son. "And I sent a letter to Mike Mammon telling him where he could stick his stupid proposal. Here's your copy." He pushed a piece of paper into his father's hand as they reached the front door. "Oh, and by the way," he said, kissing the old man on the cheek. "Happy Christmas!" He steered a surprised Mr Christmas into the house and shut the door behind him.

"What on earth did you say to the boy?" asked Mr Christmas.

It was an hour later. Mr Christmas had wallowed in his bath until the water had turned cold and his toes were as shrivelled as crinkle-cut chips. Now, wearing only a pink towel, he was standing next to his wife at the bedroom window, watching Mudrick chopping logs for the generator.

"I told him that if he didn't like the way we did things, he could leave," said Mrs Christmas.

"Oh," muttered Mr Christmas uneasily. He was wise enough to know that sometimes talking tough got results, but he didn't like being tough and wasn't very good at it.

Mudrick glanced up at his parents and waved. They waved back, but Mr Christmas's vigorous arm movement set off a ripple effect and before he could grab the towel it had slipped to the floor. While he hastily picked it up again, Mudrick gestured towards the kitchen.

"Can I see you for a minute?" he mouthed. "I'll make you a cup of tea."

"What does he want now?" asked Mr Christmas, leaning towards his wife for a kiss.

"No!" said Gertie playfully, slipping out of his grasp and slapping his tummy so hard that his towel slipped down again.

Mudrick pushed two cups of tea across the kitchen table followed by a brown envelope.

"Open it," he said to his mystified parents.

Mrs Christmas leant forward and picked it up.

"No, actually, no, before you do" – Mudrick smiled – "I just want to say that I know I haven't always been the best son, but I am grateful for everything you've done for me and this is my way of saying thank you."

The old couple were good at handing out surprises, but not so good at receiving them. Mrs Christmas's hand shook with excitement as she slit open the envelope and pulled out three tickets.

"One of them's for Custard," said Mudrick.

"Oh, Mudrick!" she gasped. "My dear boy. Theo, he's bought us a year's holiday in Herne Bay!"

"Where?" said Mr Christmas.

"Oh, stop being difficult, Theo. You know exactly where it is. It's the perfect place to get away from it all. Nothing ever happens there! Oh, I'm so happy I think I might faint!"

"But, Gertie," said Mr Christmas, "we can't possibly go."

"Why not?" Mrs Christmas shook her head in disbelief.

"Mudrick, I'm so sorry," said his father, "but we can't leave the factory for a whole year. Who will organize the presents for next Christmas?"

"No problem," said Mudrick, pointing to the tickets. "Your return flight brings you back on Christmas Eve. Everything will be ready for the present drop just like normal."

"But who will make the toys and answer the letters?"

"Dad," said Mudrick, "do you really think I haven't thought of that? Tobin, Tank, Rudolph and Papagrolin will organize everything, and I'll pop back from college to keep an eye on things. There's nothing to worry about. You both deserve a break."

There was a pause while the old man wrestled with his conscience. As Father Christmas, he had the ultimate responsibility to keep Christmas alive. What would happen if something went wrong? But it wouldn't … would it? It couldn't … could it? No. Not with Tobin and Papagrolin in charge. And Rudolph was a sensible chap.

"What can I say?" he said.

"Whatever it is, I wish you'd just say it!" said his wife.

"Very well," he said gleefully. "Where are my swimmers?"

And so it was that two days later a hot-air balloon landed in the white field beyond the cottage, and Mr and Mrs Christmas, Custard and several pieces of luggage were tossed aboard. Custard was so scared that the pilot insisted he wear mittens, to stop his claws from puncturing the balloon.

Mr Christmas was a bundle of nerves. No matter how often Mudrick reassured him that everything was fine and that Christmas was safe in his hands, his father didn't really believe him. Even while the ground ropes were being untied, Mr Christmas was full of last-minute advice for his son.

"Don't forget to keep the generator burning," he cried, "and if a child asks for something you've never heard of, write back and ask them to draw you a picture. But Tobin knows that. Oh yes, and grease the sleigh's runners once a month and don't let the reindeer eat cake. They'll get fat. And no live pets, because they're impossible to wrap. Look after Pots, feed Tank and don't be too hard on Papagrolin if he sleeps through the afternoon—"

"Oh, do be quiet!" said Mrs Christmas, clamping her hand over her husband's mouth. "I hope you're not going to be this unrelaxed for the next year. Mudrick knows what he has to do, Theo. Now leave him alone."

"All advice gratefully received!" said Mudrick as the pilot fired up the burner and the basket scraped off the ground.

"This is your mother's first time flying, you know," Mr Christmas shouted over the roar.

"I know!" Mudrick shouted back. "That's why I booked the balloon. It's *her* treat!"

Mr Christmas laughed and Mrs Christmas blew her son a kiss. "Goodbye," she cried. "Don't forget to eat!"

"And don't do anything I wouldn't do," bellowed Mr Christmas as they sailed into the clouds, with Custard clinging on for dear life.

"Actually," muttered Mudrick slyly, still smiling and waving like a dutiful son, "that's rather the idea!"

CHAPTER EIGHT

No sooner had the hot-air balloon disappeared over the horizon than Mudrick called a meeting in the courtyard. He ran upstairs to his bedroom and flung open the window. From here he could address the crowd of elves and reindeer with all the panache of a military dictator. Gone was the loving boy who had waved goodbye to his parents just minutes before. In his place stood a self-seeking young man with cold, ruthless eyes.

"So," he declaimed. "A year. My father has gone on holiday for one whole year. When he told me he'd booked this holiday I was stunned. I mean, I know a few other people who'd like a holiday too. Those people who *do all the work* around here, for example."

The crowd murmured. Mudrick had touched a nerve. It was true what he was saying.

"Somehow it doesn't seem right that *he* gets

rewarded for *your* effort, does it? But I guess that's life, and I respect your loyalty for saying nothing about it."

It was a clever start. Mudrick made it sound as if Mr Christmas deserved their loyalty, and this made Mudrick sound loyal too.

"I mean, let's face it, without you lot there wouldn't be a Father Christmas." Mudrick took a deep breath. "Call me old-fashioned," he said slowly, "but I think you should be better rewarded – you know, more money, that sort of thing."

The courtyard filled with whispering as the elves and reindeer realized that something was afoot.

"So here's my plan." Mudrick grinned. "As of now I am abandoning my education and will devote my time to rebuilding the business."

"Business?" cried Papagrolin.

"I want you to think of me as the new Father Christmas!" declared Mudrick.

"What?" shouted Rudolph. "No, no, no! Mr Christmas *is* Father Christmas. There can never be another."

But the crowd only had ears for Mudrick.

"Forget everything you've ever learnt about the spirit of Christmas," he went on, thumping the window sill. "My father has had his day. Out with the old, in with the new!"

A few of the faces in the crowd looked uneasy – Papagrolin, Rudolph and Dasher had promised Mr Christmas that nothing would change in his absence.

"Listen," said Mudrick, pointing to the elves, "if I could promise *you* that you'd work fewer hours, would you be interested?"

A shout of "Yes!" exploded from the courtyard.

"And if I could promise *you* wall-to-wall television," he said to the reindeer, "and that you'd never have to drag a sleigh across the sky again, would *you* be interested?"

Blitzen, Comet, Dancer, Donner, Prancer and Vixen thumped their hooves.

"That's impossible," shouted Rudolph. "You can't deliver presents without a magic sleigh."

"Have you never heard of postmen?" replied Mudrick.

At this the crowd laughed so much that Papagrolin had to raise his voice to make himself heard. "But the stamps will cost a fortune," he bellowed.

"Yes, they will," said Mudrick, grinning, "which is why, from now on, children will be *paying* for their presents from Father Christmas! It's going to make us all very rich!"

"Even me?" asked Pots.

"Even you," roared Mudrick. "You can buy yourself a brain, Pots!"

The laughter swelled as reindeer and elves joined together in an impromptu dance that involved a lot of hugging and even more jumping up and down on the spot.

"We need never work again!" cried Sealeater.

But not everyone thought that this was a good thing.

"I quite like work," Dasher whispered to Rudolph.

"We're going to call ourselves fatherchrist-mas.com and sell Santa cheap on the Internet," declared Mudrick. "It's easy! We'll buy a computer, make a few toys, take a few orders by email, stick on a few stamps, then sit back and wait for the money to roll in!"

"And how are we going to pay for a computer?" challenged Rudolph.

"One man's junk is another man's treasure," said Mudrick, pointing to the reject pile of broken toys that Father Christmas destroyed every new year. Only this year Mudrick had told his father to leave that job to him.

When a Japanese whaling ship ran aground on an iceberg, Mudrick took the opportunity to hold a garage sale of all the trashy presents in Father Christmas's reject pile. Three hundred sailors snapped up the bargains and left the rest for a man with impossibly white teeth and a sparkling suit.

"Lars Thorsen. Swedish TV," he said. "We're looking for cheap prizes for a new daytime game show. Can you help?"

Mudrick chucked the boomall/ballerang into the Swede's hands and slapped him on the shoulder.

"Lars!" he declared with a grin. "Unbuckle that wallet!"

Mudrick had his cash. Now for the computer.

CHAPTER NINE

Mr and Mrs Christmas landed on the championship green of the Herne Bay Over Seventies Bowling Club. Their balloon caused quite a stir, not least to the bowls on the green at the time. Nobody had ever seen a balloon before in Herne Bay, so the bowlers assumed that Mr and Mrs Christmas were very posh indeed.

They think we're royalty!

wrote Mrs Christmas in her first postcard home, to let Mudrick know that they'd arrived safely.

And we don't want them knowing who we really are, so Custard's pretending to be a corgi!

Then she drew a picture of Custard barking and standing on his knees to look shorter.

Their room at the Sea View Hotel, a bed and breakfast establishment, had a perfect view of grey skies, grey seas and grey pebbled beaches. Mrs Christmas loved it. It took Mr Christmas a little longer to settle because, no matter how hard he tried to switch off from work, he couldn't stop worrying about the toy factory at the North Pole!

Dear Mudrick,

Wish you were here.

Love

Dad

PS How is the factory going? Any letters in yet for next year? Have you started making presents yet? Is Tank keeping the furnace alight? Has the sleigh been stripped and polished? Paper to answer letters in drawer of kitchen table ... with pencils. And don't let the reindeer get fat!

Dear Mum and Dad,

Best thing you've ever done - going on holiday. It makes me so happy to know that you're not here! Everything running smoothly. Logs have just arrived. Hope I ordered enough! College hunky-dory!

Love

Mudrick

PS Everyone getting on like a house on fire.

But everyone was *not* getting on like a house on fire. The elves were divided on the question of clothing. The majority wanted to ditch their traditional costumes in favour of more comfortable clothes like trainers and jeans. But the night they burnt their lederhosen and danced naked around the bonfire, Papagrolin and Pots did not join in. Papagrolin wanted no part of this childish tomfoolery. Pots, on the other hand, just liked his leather shorts. They were snug. He didn't *want* to change them. Besides, now that he had his goblin computer game to keep him amused, the one Mudrick had so nonchalantly discarded, Pots didn't mix much with the other elves any more. He spent all of his time in the mystical cyberworld of Gandor the Goblin King.

As for the reindeer, they were divided too. The rest of the team refused to speak to Dasher and

Rudolph because they dared to suggest that nude moonbathing was not an appropriate activity for a magic reindeer.

Mudrick was far too busy setting up father-christmas.com to notice these potentially dangerous splits in his workforce. His biggest problem was tracking down a computer big enough to handle the quantity of emails he was expecting. He was starting to despair, when Blitzen came across a company in the phone book called morecomputersthananyothercomputercompanyintheknownuniverseandbeyond.com.

"Hello," said the sales rep at the other end of the phone. "Morecomputersthananyothercomputercompanyintheknownuniverseandbeyond.com. How may I help you?"

Mudrick was sitting in the kitchen. "I'm looking for a big computer," he said. "Have you got one?"

"How big's big?" asked the salesman.

"Big!" said Mudrick. Mudrick liked big. Big was powerful and that was how Mudrick saw himself. "It has to handle traffic from every single child in the world."

"Jeepers!" exclaimed the sales rep. "In that case you'll be needing our top-of-the-range model, sir."

"Is it heavy on the RAM?" checked Mudrick.

"Oh yes, sir," came the reply. "Lots of RAM. Masses of megabytes, gigabytes and tastybytes, expansion ports, memories, modems, zips and floppies, plus speakers, scanners, printers, web cams, CPUs, DVDs, RUWithMes and a mouse."

"Excellent!" trilled Mudrick.

"But," said the sales rep, sounding an unexpected warning, "it is BIG, as I've said, and it does need a big table to sit on."

With one sweep of his arm Mudrick brushed his parents' belongings off the kitchen table to create some space.

"No problem," he shouted, raising his voice over the noise of smashing china. "I'll take it!"

"Just one more thing, sir."

Mudrick held his breath. "Don't tell me," he said, flustered. "They're in short supply. You can't get me one till after next Christmas."

"No, sir. But to keep this big computer running, you'll need a big supply of electricity as well."

Dear Mudrick,

Thank you for putting my mind at rest. I was relieved to hear that you had ordered the logs for the generator. Now that I know Father Christmas is in safe hands I can start to relax. I have just been for my first walk. Your mother and I took Custard on the beach. Unfortunately we had to come back early when he was chased by a hermit crab!

Love
Dad

Making sure there was a big supply of electricity became Mudrick's priority. He turned to Tank, the strongest elf by a metric ton, but also the hungriest. Tank informed Mudrick that he would need a little encouragement to keep the furnace stoked, so Mudrick sent out for a box of salted fish, which he then fed to the giant elf on a reward-only basis. Tank was only given food after he had filled the furnace with logs. Like a trainer feeding a sea lion, Mudrick dangled a stinking fish above Tank's nose until he agreed to Mudrick's demands.

"All right, I'll do it!" screamed the tortured elf. "So long as I've got logs, I'll give you as much electricity as you want for the factory and your stupid new computer!"

"Thank you," said Mudrick, dropping the whole fish down Tank's extendable gullet. Then, as Tank digested his meal with all the delicacy of a killer whale, Mudrick pushed his madcap money-making scheme one step closer to completion.

"Tobin," he said, "spread the word! It's toy time!"

The factory chugged back to life, only this time, instead of making billions of different toys – a different toy for every child in the world – Mudrick made six.

Pots protested on behalf of all children everywhere. "What happens if a child doesn't want one of the six presents on offer?" he asked.

"They'll take what they're given!" said Mudrick.

"But what if they won't?"

"Then they'll go without!" he said. "I'm interested in their money, Pots, not their happiness!"

So, while Tank picked fish bones out of his teeth, the factory churned out Mudrick's six presents. They weren't special presents, obviously; they were basic presents of the boring kind that children only buy when the one they already own has worn out – a ball, a bat, a doll, a gun, pyjamas and a pair of white socks.

There was a sign over the factory door that Mr Christmas had painted himself to keep the elves on their toes and remind them why they were there. It was a simple message.

Remember!
Every child must get the
present they asked for.

Mudrick tore it down and threw it in the furnace. A different present for every child was too much like hard work. And when laziness meant that toys came off the production line damaged, Mudrick refused to throw them away. Papagrolin complained.

"Your father would never allow such tat to leave the factory," he said.

"I'm not my father!" snapped Mudrick.

"No," sniffed the senior elf. "That much is obvious. If you were, you'd know that Father Christmas can't give every child the same present. It destroys the magic."

"Who cares?" Mudrick laughed. "We'll have their money in the bank before the presents ever arrive."

"But it's Christmas! The most exciting day of a child's year."

"It's big bucks," said Mudrick. "That's the vision, old man. Take it or leave it!"

Papagrolin left it.

"Your father would be heartbroken," he said pointedly as he turned his back and walked away.

Production continued for months until the elves were sick of the sight of balls, bats, dolls, guns, pyjamas and white socks. They wanted to stop, but being a novice Father Christmas Mudrick didn't know how many presents he would need.

"As many presents as there are children in the world," said Tobin.

"And how many's that?" asked Mudrick.

The exhausted elf stared wearily at the huge pile of single white socks that still needed folding into pairs.

"Too many," he sighed.

The elves were not exactly unhappy, but they did wonder when Mudrick's promised life of luxury was going to begin.

The following week, Tank reported a shortage of logs and Mudrick flew into a rage. It was his mistake: he had ordered too few and this was the North Pole where there wasn't a tree for hundreds of miles. Without the generator to power his big computer when it arrived, fatherchristmas.com was doomed to failure before it even started. Finding an alternative source of fuel was suddenly Mudrick's priority.

In a school in Uganda, built out of mud and clay, a classroom of children were writing letters to Father Christmas. They always sent them early in the year, because Africa to the North Pole is a long long way. A young girl called Kassalina had been looking forward to writing her first letter to Father Christmas ever since she could remember. Now she had started school she was about to realize her dream – to write to the magic man in the sleigh and receive a present from the sky!

DeaR FatheR ChRistmas,
   Hello. I am gud all yeer. I am neaRly seven. I hav bewtiful black haiR and a momy and dady hoo aRe nice. I am so loking foRwaRd to ChRistmas and suRpRises. Plese can I have a pensil case foR skool, becoz evRy other one has got one and not me. Mum sayz we iz two pooR, but we iz not two pooR to hav a pensil case.
   Love yu
   Kassalina

Papagrolin read Kassalina's letter to Rudolph, Dasher and Pots by the green glow that radiated from the screen of Pots's computer game. They were meeting secretly in the stables.

"Of course you must reply," whispered Rudolph.

"But Mudrick has forbidden it," said Papagrolin. "He's instructed me to chuck all the letters in the shed."

"Must we do everything Mudrick says?" asked Rudolph.

A sudden noise caught their attention.

"I'm afraid so," said Mudrick, stepping out of the shadows where he'd been hiding. He snatched the letter out of Papagrolin's hands. "And there's nothing you can do about it!"

CHAPTER TEN

A few weeks later the logs ran out. Mudrick was composing another lie to his parents at the time. Mr and Mrs Christmas had joined the Herne Bay Over Seventies Bowling Club and were having more fun with their new-found friends than they would have thought possible. Mr Christmas's latest postcard recounted a hilarious incident when he knelt down to deliver a bowl and trod on his beard by mistake. The ensuing tumble had caused such mirth and merriment amongst the players that the game had been abandoned in favour of sweet sherries all round in the clubhouse!

...So, do you think bowls might catch on with youngsters instead of skateboarding? If so, start making bowling balls immediately and put a footnote in the rule book warning men with long beards to take extra care!

Love

Dad and Mum

Mudrick was just writing back:

Dear Mum and Dad,

You're so down with the kids, it's scary. Of course youngsters will love bowling. When have you ever been wrong? I'm on to it yester

when the lights went out and the kitchen was plunged into darkness. He stood up from the table and opened the front door. Outside, the moonlit courtyard was eerily quiet; there was just the faint whistle of an Arctic wind. The generator had stopped.

Mudrick ran across the courtyard and circled round to the rear of the factory, where he found Tank sitting with his back against the wall, mouth wide open, preparing to eat a squid sandwich.

"Tank!" shouted Mudrick. "What is going on? We've lost power."

The giant elf was so surprised at the interruption

that he dropped both pieces of bread, and the squid slopped away.

"The logs are finished," he said as Tobin rushed out of the gloom to see what the problem was.

"Right," said Mudrick, "clear thinking required. No more toys, Tobin. The factory is now officially closed. We'll make do with what we've got already."

Tobin smiled. "Good news," he said. "The elves will be pleased."

"Some children will just have to go without toys," said Mudrick. "And when the computer arrives we'll need to find something else to burn. I suggest you start looking, Tank."

But Tank wasn't looking for anything other than his sandwich filling. He had already disappeared into the snowfields in hot pursuit of a buttered-up squid.

While the factory lay idle and the elves enjoyed a relaxing curling tournament, the reindeer were hitched up to the sleigh and told to fly round and round the world with an advertising banner in tow. Or, more accurately, all the reindeer except Rudolph and Dasher, who refused to do anything to help fatherchristmas.com become a success. Losing two runners, and front-runners at that, left the sleigh seriously underpowered and the remaining reindeer were not pleased.

"We only went along with your plan because you told us it would mean an end to exhausting flights around the world," argued Vixen. "Now look what we're doing!"

"This is the last time, I promise," said Mudrick.

"You're letting the world know that we're here. You're selling us. If you don't do it we might as well pack up now, call Dad home from Herne Bay and wave goodbye to our fortunes."

The mention of lost fortunes was the clincher.

Reluctantly and with very bad grace the six lazy reindeer lumbered into the field and prepared for take-off. None of them would fly lead so the two front positions stayed empty, which made steering twice as hard. They trundled up the runway all right, but when an extra effort was needed to lift the sleigh off the ground they couldn't produce it. The sleigh hopped and slid and bounced and slewed until eventually it flipped over in a forward somersault and skidded to a halt upside down.

"That was pathetic!" shouted Mudrick.

"It's not our fault," complained Prancer. "We need the extra oomph from Rudolph and Dasher!"

"Well, you can whistle for it!" Dasher said to the harnessed reindeer. "I don't agree with what you're doing, do I, Rudolph?"

"No, Dasher, you don't," replied Rudolph, shouting to ram home his point. "You think they're TURNCOATS and SCOUNDRELS!" Then he lowered his voice and smiled politely. "You'll just have to go oomphless, I'm afraid."

"Why don't Blitzen and Vixen move to the front?" said Pots, a sensible suggestion that met with a hostile response.

"Put a sock in it!" hollered Vixen. "I always said you were trouble, Pots!"

"He's right," Mudrick said firmly. "You two always go for the easy ride. Do it!"

Blitzen and Vixen were flabbergasted by Mudrick's aggressive tone.

"I beg your pardon?" said Vixen.

"DO IT!" ordered Mudrick. He was not coming this far to be thwarted by a couple of work-shy reindeer.

"Now hang on one min—" protested Blitzen, but Mudrick shut him up for good by jamming a postcard in his mouth.

"And while you're up there," he said, smiling, "pop that in the post for Mum and Dad, will you?"

Ten minutes later, the talismanic motor in full hum, the magic sleigh took off from the snowfield with Blitzen and Vixen puffing and blowing at the front.

"This is a really *bad* idea," panted Vixen as the silver runners lifted off the snow.

The sleigh climbed through the wispy summer clouds and a huge canvas banner unfurled into the sky.

dotcom.ing soon – fatherchristmas.com

On the ice floe at the South Pole, the same family of emperor penguins stood in a line and watched the magic sleigh pass overhead. And just as they had done before, they tumbled backwards and knocked each other down like a row of dominoes. As they lay on their backs, the penguins marvelled at how quickly

Christmas had come round this year.

The reindeer flew round and round the world for three days and three nights and didn't come home until every person in every town in every country in the world had seen the banner.

Off Bondi Beach a swimmer was being chased by a great white shark when the sleigh flew overhead. The big fish spotted it first and tapped the man on the shoulder with its fin. They stopped the chase to watch it fly by.

On a Tibetan mountainside a goatherd was soothing his highly strung goats with a tune on his Tibetan horn. He got such a shock when the banner whizzed past that he swallowed the mouthpiece of the horn and spoke with a bleat for ever after.

In Florida a parade of majorettes came to a sticky end when the marching leader looked up, saw the banner and forgot to catch her metal mace. It twirled back to earth with a sickening crunch and took out rows two to six.

In India a spindly-legged boy had just burst his lungs cycling his rickshaw to the top of a steep hill when the reindeer hoofed by. The weary boy stopped pedalling and gasped in wonder, while the fat fare in the seat behind cried out in alarm. When they reached the bottom of the hill they were doing ninety miles an hour ... backwards!

Everywhere, in Paris, Rome, Cairo, Athens, Khartoum, Baghdad and Tahiti, people stopped and stared at the miracle sleigh. But in Herne Bay, England, it was a different story.

Mr and Mrs Christmas were walking Custard along the shore in a force nine gale. The horizontal rain lashed against their waterproof coats like spray from a fire hose. Thunder split the sky in two, lightning speared the sea and a quivering Custard leapt off the ground and curled himself around Mrs Christmas's neck like a fur stole. It was quite a storm!

Mrs Christmas was reading Mudrick's latest postcard. It was the one Blitzen had posted.

Trust me, Mum and Dad. The sun is very hot in Herne Bay at this time of year. Under no circumstances look up at the sky or it will blind you. OK?

Love

Mudrick

"I suppose he knows what he's talking about," she said as rain splattered the postcard and made the ink run.

"Oh, yes," said Mr Christmas. "I expect the sun will be out any minute now."

Dutifully following their son's instructions, they were both looking down at the pavement when the sleigh flew past, so they never read the banner that would have blown the whistle on Mudrick's little game. Instead Mrs Christmas found a coin on the ground.

"Oh, look, an old penny!" she exclaimed. "You

72

know what this means, don't you, Theo?"

"Yes," said her husband, kissing her lovingly on the cheek. "We are the luckiest people alive!"

And so it was that everybody in the world *except* Mr and Mrs Christmas saw the advertisement for fatherchristmas.com. Even Custard spotted it, but being a snow leopard he didn't have the words to tell them.

CHAPTER ELEVEN

When the magic sleigh returned to the North Pole the elves took off the runners, packed the seats with mothballs and bundled it away under an old tarpaulin at the back of the green hut. Under Mudrick's new dotcom regime Father Christmas had no need of a sleigh. The exhausted reindeer fell into the stables and slept for a week, at the end of which Tobin woke them up with some good news.

"Morning," he said. "It's time for your reward."

Mudrick stepped forward with a grin on his face. "You may now take the rest of your lives off!"

The reindeer were too tired to cheer. They opened their eyes for half a second, flickered a smile and went back to sleep. Only now their dreams were of all-night parties, more grass than they could eat, growing fat and lazy, and never pulling a sleigh again!

"Mr Mudrick?" It was a stranger's voice.

Mudrick swung round to see who it was.

Standing in the courtyard was a snow raft – six husky sledges lashed together to make one huge platform. It needed to be huge too, because sitting on top of the platform was a large wooden crate with the word FRAGILE stamped all over it. On one side was the name of the delivery company – morecomputersthananyothercomputercompanyintheknownuniverseandbeyond.com. The snow raft was pulled by four polar bears who were panting heavily, and driven by a young man who was now divesting himself of his warm outer garments to reveal a salesman's suit underneath. In the sunshine the shiny fabric shimmered like mirrored glass.

"I told you it was big," said the computer salesman.

Tank was crossing the courtyard heading for home.

"Coat off!" barked Mudrick.

"But I'm just going home for elevenses," complained the hungry elf.

Mudrick shook his head and pointed to the giant computer.

"We need that extra fuel," he said, "now!"

DeaR FatheR ChRistmas,

 I am now wuRRRed. I hav not huRd from yu. But I need the pensil case to stop SoRaya beeting up on me at skool. She says I am as pooR as a pig, becoz I don't have a pensil case.

Love
Kassalina

PS How can a pig be pooR if it neveR has money to begin with? Maybee sum pigs are Rich and I don't kno. Can a pig win the lottRy?

The furnace roared back into life. Tank wiped the sweat from his brow and shovelled a stack of letters into the mouth of the fiery beast. Mudrick patted Tank on the head and gave him a dog biscuit.

"Good boy," he said, snatching more letters off the pile. "I knew we'd find something useless to burn!"

Papagrolin and Rudolph, who had been watching from a distance, couldn't bear it any longer. As Kassalina's letter went up in smoke they marched forward. Rudolph kicked the shovel out of Tank's hands while Papagrolin snatched the letters from Mudrick.

"This is sacrilege!" he growled.

"These children believe in Father Christmas," said Rudolph. "You have no right to destroy their dreams!"

Mudrick was unmoved. He grabbed the letters back from Papagrolin and threw them on the fire.

"It's paper," he said. "It burns."

In the kitchen the big computer suddenly burst into life. A funky trumpet fanfare played over a blank screen, then a picture appeared. A cartoon beetle scuttled across an empty white space only to be viciously squashed by a large stamping army boot.

"Hi," said the computer's American voice. "I'm your big computer and I'm booted up!"

The elves around the table cheered and slapped Mudrick on the back. At last, here was progress. Mudrick's dream was coming true.

"It's going to happen!" he told Tobin, grabbing the elf's shoulders and pogoing up and down. "We're going to be rich!"

To help him achieve his ambition, Mudrick had enlisted the assistance of two teenage elves called Hamblatt and Poochie. By elf standards they were very cool. They wore Hawaiian shirts, army shorts, baseball caps and shades. But their real skills lay in computer graphics, in designing new games to shock and excite an unshockable market. The key to their success was blood, as any game player will tell you.

They never spilt a pint of blood where a gallon would do. The task Mudrick had set them was simple.

"Design me a new Father Christmas!"

"Any specifications?" asked Hamblatt.

"Only one," said Mudrick. "*She's* got to be sexy!"

"Sexy" took a while. Hamblatt and Poochie worked for weeks, staying up late into the night wrestling with ideas, only to throw them in the bin every morning. But slowly their vision took shape. As their design neared completion and the prospect of a television advertising campaign reared its head, Mudrick decided he'd better send his parents another postcard. His father's last note had given him cause for concern.

Dear Mudrick,

What a fool I am! All those wasted years not watching television because I thought it was dross. Was I mad? I think I was, because since we've arrived in Herne Bay I've been watching quite a bit. The other guests insist on having the telly on ALL the time. We tend to start early with a breakfast show, followed by loud cartoons, daytime chat shows, the shopping channel, several soaps, a couple of quizzes and, before bed, a rather lovely black and white film! Remind me never to say NEVER again. I must try new things in future. I've missed a whole world of excitement! Must rush as "Countdown" is on and I'm rather good at it.

Love

Dad (and Mum)

Mudrick's reply arrived at the Sea View Hotel during the nail-biting finale of a DIY makeover. Mrs Christmas walked into the television lounge and waved the postcard at her husband.

"Another one from Mudrick, Theo," she said.

Mr Christmas did not even look up. He was too busy watching paint dry.

"There was a time," said his wife pointedly, "*before* television, when you used to talk to me."

"Sorry." Mr Christmas yawned. "I'm feeling a bit sleepy."

"Well, the adverts are on in a minute," said Mrs Christmas. "You always wake up for those."

"I like adverts." Mr Christmas chuckled. "All those dogs in hats. They're funny!" Then he turned back to the screen, while Mrs Christmas read Mudrick's postcard.

Mum! Dad! STOP! Dad was right all along! Scientists have just published new research proving BEYOND DOUBT that television programmes are awful. Every programme kills off a million brain cells, because it is so dreary. If you watch TV your brain will shrink from exposure to too much rubbish and you will die very soon, especially if you are old, which you are. So SWITCH IT OFF or DIE!

80

Mrs Christmas gasped and blinked at the television in frozen panic. Then in a moment of quick thinking she grabbed the teapot off the tea tray and hurled it at the screen, much to the astonishment of the other guests.

"I was watching that!" complained Mr Christmas as the black box fizzled and steamed. "It was an advert about Christmas."

It wasn't just any old advert about Christmas. It was Mudrick's advert for fatherchristmas.com. By the skin of his teeth the cunning freckle-faced boy had once again kept his plan secret from his parents. At the same time he was managing to pump the name of fatherchristmas.com into every sitting room in every home in the world. Only time would tell if the world was going to listen or not.

The advert started with a sweet rendition of "Jingle Bells" tinkling over a chocolate-box scene of a cosy little cottage shrouded in falling snow. A robin sang on a holly twig, a snowman smiled behind a fence, and two wonder-struck children sat at an upstairs window scouring the sky for their first glimpse of Father Christmas. There! What was that? Over there, behind that star…

Suddenly a pointed stiletto heel tore through the pretty picture like a sharp knife through canvas, while the tinkling music was swallowed up by a tidal surge of rock guitars. Gone was the Christmas cottage. Bubbling lava poured down a street littered with white-hot rocks and smoking ash. Wearing top-to-toe black leathers, a motorcyclist roared

81

towards the camera on a Harley-Davidson, skidded out of a wheelie and screeched to a halt. The rider tore off the catsuit and helmet and shook out her long hair. It was a girl!

"Hi, boys," she drawled in a come-hither Texan accent. She had curves like an hourglass and a saucy pouting mouth, and was wearing a short red dress trimmed with white fur, white fishnet stockings and high-heeled boots. She had a Uzi sub-machine gun strapped across her shoulder and a bowie knife in her belt.

"Father Christmas has hung up his boots and retired to bed," she purred in a voice like melted toffee. "From now on, if you want to celebrate Christmas, you're going to have to celebrate it with me, his badass daughter, Lara Christmas!"

Gone were the baggy red suit and the heavy black boots. Gone were the long white beard and yo-ho-ho laugh. In his place Hamblatt and Poochie had invented Lara Christmas, Father Christmas's foxy daughter!

The camera cut in close and focused on her lips. "I love you!" she whispered. "And if you love Christmas there's only one place to be – father-christmas.com." Then she winked and blew the viewer a kiss. "See you under the mistletoe!"

Mudrick and all of the elves except Papagrolin and Pots watched the first broadcast on a television in the kitchen. Mudrick could not contain his excitement. As Lara blew that kiss at the end, he leapt off his chair and punched the air.

82

"You bet, sweetheart!" he screamed at the screen, throwing his arms around Tobin and giving him a kiss. "I don't know about anyone else but I feel 'rich' coming on! Hamblatt, Poochie..." He called the designer whizz-kids over to his side. "What you two have done is beautiful!" He slapped them both on the shoulder. "And what all of us are about to do together will not only be beautiful, but historic too!" Then he pointed to the computer. "Let's do it, guys! Let's go online!"

Fatherchristmas.com was on the verge of existence. A flick of a switch here, a six-button sequence there, a double click, Return, Enter and POW! The screen exploded into life and fatherchristmas.com, the world's first sleighless Santa website, was open for business!

Outside, it stopped snowing.

When they first logged on to the site visitors were greeted by a night sky twinkling with iridescent stars. In the distance Father Christmas's sleigh was carving an arc across the sky. Suddenly Lara Christmas sprang into the foreground and shot it down with a flame-thrower. Then she turned, with the crippled sleigh still burning behind her.

"So you found me," she simpered as a flashing sign appeared just below her chin.

No more letters to Father Christmas   Emails only to
larachristmas@fatherchristmas.com

"Welcome to fatherchristmas.com, one-stop stocking shopping! Hit me!" By pressing the cursor on the money symbol the desktop helper sprang into life. It was a wad of talking money.

"Hi," it said. "Money talks, so that's me! Double click on the money icon to go directly to our wide range of six toys available now."

With a tacky trumpet fanfare the screen rotated to reveal the six gorgeous presents available on fatherchristmas.com. They sparkled in their red tinsel boxes like prizes on a goldfish stall at the funfair.

1. BALL • 155 crowns

2. DOLL • 225 crowns

3. fatherchristmas.com NICE WHITE SOCKS (1 PAIR) • 98 crowns

4. fatherchristmas.com PYJAMAS • 135 crowns

5. TOY GUN • 210 crowns

6. BAT • 165 crowns

Then the screen was bombarded with spinning captions and flashing prices. "Never have toys been so CHEAP!" said the money wad. "Simply click on the item you require, then enter your name, postcode and credit card number." CREDIT CARD NUMBER flashed urgently in the viewer's face, followed by several helpful reminders.

Remember, these superb products are not available in the shops.

No refunds!

Please note • batteries, bulbs, nuts, bolts, screws, nails, instructions, glue, thread and paint are NOT included. An additional charge of 22.50 crowns per item will secure these extra parts.

P • P costs an additional 4.45 crowns per item or 444.45 crowns per item outside the North Pole.

Guaranteed delivery in forty-nine days.

And it all finished up with a sign-off from Lara herself, tastefully captioned LARA'S BIG END.

"Remember," she said. "Father Christmas is no longer available. Buy now while stocks last!"

If your item is out of stock, we will
provide another item as closely matched
to the ordered item as possible, or NOT,
depending on what is still available.

HAPPY CHRISTMAS!

CHAPTER TWELVE

It was five forty-five on a blustery evening in Herne Bay and all was quiet. In the front room of the Sea View Hotel the guests were enjoying a peaceful evening of home entertainment. Most of them were staring at the cracked teapot lodged inside the shattered screen of the television set, but Mrs Christmas and Custard were playing a cut-throat game of cards in the alcove.

"Fish!" said Mrs Christmas. "My go."

There was a thud and a curse in the corridor outside, then the door burst open and a red-faced Mr Christmas staggered into the room carrying a weighty cardboard box.

"Make way!" he cried. "Can't stop. Too heavy!"

He rushed to the sofa, where he fell over and dropped the box onto the cushions. Then he undid the top flaps to show his fellow guests what he'd bought.

"Oooh!" they all gasped. "A new television!"

Mrs Christmas was amazed. Her husband was a creature of habit. He *never* changed his ways. Yet here he was not just watching television, but *buying* one too!

It had been a while since Mudrick had launched his website. Since then there had been only disappointment. Many had visited the site, but none had bought. The unwanted presents were piled up outside in the snow getting colder and damper by the day. The nice white socks had turned green with mould, and disillusioned emails, like this one from Kassalina, had become the norm.

```
Hello again FatheR
ChRistmas. Kassalina heRe.
At last I have fowned you.
On InteRnet. But it iz LaRa
your doRter not you. What
hoRRible pResents. Plese
put pensil case on list oR
I will be veRy sad.
   Love
   Kassalina
```

Mudrick's plan to turn old rope into money was fraying at the edges. If nobody bought his presents, he would go bankrupt before Christmas.

"I don't understand," he screamed at the kitchen walls. "All we're getting are complaints. Why won't they buy?"

But people were not prepared to pay for presents that used to be free, especially when they were so tacky.

So the spirit of Christmas started to wither on the vine. Where once there had been excitement, expectation, wonder and surprise, now, all of a sudden, there was nothing. By stealing Father Christmas, Mudrick had stolen the magic from the world.

In an effort to combat consumer lethargy, Mudrick asked Hamblatt and Poochie to produce a series of shocking adverts to grab the public's attention. They came up with three.

The first had Lara pointing a gun at a Christmas fairy's head.

"Come to fatherchristmas.com," she instructed the viewer, "or the fairy gets it!"

The second had Lara spinning out of a tree with a crossbow. She hit the ground and fired at the camera. Then it cut to her posing like a great white hunter on the corpse of a magic reindeer with a bright red nose.

"There's nothing dear at fatherchristmas.com. Log on," she said straight down the lens, "or else!"

The third saw Lara skiing through an alpine

forest behind a pack of wild huskies baying for blood.

"We know where you live," she threatened in true Mafia style. "And if you don't buy-buy from us, we'll say bye-bye to you!"

In early December Mudrick, Sealeater and Tobin watched the adverts go out on a portable television set that Mudrick had bought for the reindeer. They had installed it in their field but reception was bad, so Dasher's antlers had been volunteered as a TV aerial. His job, once wired into the back of the set, was to contort his body into ever more twisted shapes in order to find a position that maximized picture quality. Right now he was teetering on three legs and touching his tail with his nose.

"That's it!" shouted Donner. "Don't move!"

Mudrick, Sealeater and Tobin were trying to work out why the adverts weren't having an effect. In the last week the website had attracted only three visitors and none of them had stayed.

"Maybe the adverts are too violent," suggested Tobin, "and they're putting people off."

"Nonsense," said Mudrick. "Kids love violence. If anything the ads are too soft. No, we're missing a trick somewhere."

"Maybe we should ask the reindeer what they think," said Sealeater. "See if they've got any ideas."

Mudrick laughed. "The reindeer don't think," he whispered. "Look at them. They're four-legged bimbos. All they're interested in is having a good time."

Ever since their last ride, the reindeer had lived the life of Riley out in the snowfields. Comet and Dancer spent all day stretched out on moon-loungers, slapping on factor four, wearing moon-glasses and drinking cloverleaf cocktails. Donner put his hooves up and watched wall-to-wall horse racing on the telly, and Vixen and Blitzen played antlerball, a rather slow game in which two players faced one another over a high net and tried to head the ball past each other using only their antlers. When balls burst, which they did with *every* shot, Vixen and Blitzen simply nicked another ball from the stock of fatherchristmas.com presents, until there was not a single one left.

"What are we going to tell Mudrick?" whispered Blitzen nervously. He still had a punctured ball skewered on his antler.

"Nothing," said Vixen. "Nobody wants to buy anything anyway."

Prancer made himself a sequinned tutu and spent his days practising demi-pliés and entrechats on the five-bar gate. But like all the others he soon grew fat on the plentiful supplies of grass and cream cakes, and after a while he couldn't even jump off the ground let alone fit into his tutu.

No, asking the reindeer why fatherchristmas.com was failing would have been a complete waste of time!

Then, one week before Christmas, the world woke up and protested.

THE LAST NOEL?

Today greed has destroyed Christmas. Billions of people all over the world have refused to celebrate the annual holiday while a dotcom whizz-kid is holding them to ransom. Mudrick Christmas, the founder of fatherchristmas.com, denies hijacking a public holiday for personal gain, but faced with the choice of paying for Father Christmas's services or sacrificing Christmas by way of protest, people have chosen the path of non-festivity. Christmas has been cancelled.

The newspapers roared their opposition to what Mudrick was trying to do, while millions of people watched an unprecedented global news bulletin, in which outraged national leaders officially declared Christmas cancelled. Prime ministers and presidents condemned fatherchristmas.com as just another dot*con*, an act of tinsel terrorism that would *never* succeed. The report showed that ordinary people were making their voices heard too by simply saying no. In Denmark huge piles of Christmas trees were burnt while their decorations still twinkled. In London a team of men with bolt cutters and chainsaws cut down the lights over Regent Street. In the sun-baked streets of Honolulu they banned fake snow. Mudrick was labelled "the greediest man alive" by the Queen of England, who made a special Not The Queen's Speech, which finished with a heartfelt plea.

"If you are the real Father Christmas," she said, "please return from wherever you are and put the magic back into Christmas. We thank you."

In a small brown lounge in Herne Bay a white-haired old couple were struck dumb by what they had just seen on the television news. They sat in silence staring at Mr Christmas's photograph on the screen and tried to come to terms with the fact that their own son had betrayed them.

The other guests of the Sea View Hotel sat staring at Mr and Mrs Christmas. They had never seen celebrities this close up before. It was amazing – they talked, they walked, they played Fish! Suddenly the excitement was too much and a teacup smashed.

"Gertie," said Mr Christmas, coming out of his daze. "We're going home."

Ten minutes later, Mr and Mrs Christmas bustled into the Herne Bay post office to send two urgent messages. One to Mudrick at the North Pole and one to the pilot of the hot-air balloon asking him to pick them up immediately and fly them home. But this was Herne Bay, a town where smoke signals were the cutting edge of communications technology.

"So the phones aren't working, you don't send telegrams, and you're waiting for stamps to be delivered?"

"That's right. We're a post office," said the deaf old lady behind the counter. "I've got some rainbow drops."

"No," said Mr Christmas. "Do you do those he-mail things?"

"He-what?" she said, thumping her faulty hearing aid.

"Look, this is urgent," explained Mrs Christmas. "We have to get home quickly and let our son know we're coming."

"Before he does any more damage," said Mr Christmas ruefully.

"We've got a carrier pigeon," said the old lady, plonking a rather fat pigeon on the counter.

"No," sighed a frustrated Mr Christmas, who in

the spirit of "Never say *never* again" was, for the first time in his life, prepared to place his trust in computers if they could get him home. "You send hemails by cybersky or something. On the Inter-whatsit. Look, I don't know how they work; I just know that they're fast!"

"Is that right?" said the assistant, patting her purple hair back into place. "Next you'll be telling me they can put a man on the moon."

In Herne Bay the Internet would not make an appearance for at least another fifty years, and poor old Mr and Mrs Christmas would just have to twiddle their thumbs and fret until the balloon arrived to take them home as planned on Christmas Eve.

In a snowfield at the North Pole the elves and reindeer had just watched the same news bulletin on their television – everyone except Dasher, of course, whose aerial duties forbade him from moving in case the picture went wonky. After the Queen had spoken, all eyes turned to Mudrick.

"Look, I know what you're thinking," he said. "It's less than a week to Christmas, we haven't sold a single toy and now the world hates us! But you've got to look on the bright side."

"Which is?" said Papagrolin.

Mudrick paused, scratched his top lip and tried to think of something positive to say about fatherchristmas.com. He sensed that mutiny was imminent. Whatever he said, he had better say it soon and make it good.

"Mudrick!" Hamblatt and Poochie came screaming out of the cottage waving their arms. "We've just made a sale!"

For a second Mudrick froze in disbelief, then his face burst into a broad smile.

"Yes!" he roared. "I knew I could do it!" And, realizing that this was just the tonic he needed to raise everyone's spirits and keep them on his side, he yelled out, "This calls for a celebration. Let's party!"

As everyone rushed off to whoop it up, Blitzen grabbed Hamblatt by the shirt and asked him what had been sold.

"A ball!" screamed Hamblatt. "A ball! I never knew a ball could be so exciting!"

Or so flat, thought Blitzen guiltily. Maybe antlerball hadn't been such a good idea after all.

That night, while the North Pole rocked, the first and last order for fatherchristmas.com was cancelled when Blitzen posted a notice on the website that read:

BALLS ARE OFF!

But the party went on regardless.

CHAPTER THIRTEEN

Three days later it was Christmas Eve. The sky roared as a widening shadow raced across the snow and a balloon landed in the field behind the stables. The bottom of the basket skipped across the ground then tipped over and was dragged through the snow until it juddered to a halt. The balloon sank to the ground with a deathly sigh as Custard leapt out of the upturned basket, shook the snow off his back, then turned and waited for Mr and Mrs Christmas to follow.

"Mudrick!" roared Mr Christmas as he crawled out from under the basket. "MUDRICK! WHERE ARE YOU?"

He stood up and scanned the cluster of buildings for signs of life, while behind him Mrs Christmas was still trying to disembark.

"Theo," she called.

Mr Christmas turned round to find his wife

jammed in the rigging, hanging upside down from her boots.

"Don't move a muscle," he said, unfastening her laces. Her feet slipped out of her boots and she crashed to the ground.

"Hello!" called Mrs Christmas as they struggled into the deserted courtyard, dragging their luggage behind them. "Isn't it quiet?" she whispered. It was like a ghost town.

Mr Christmas peered through the open doors into the hut where the magic sleigh had been mothballed. "Bother!" he muttered. "Bother, bother, BOTHER!"

"The factory's stopped working," said Mrs Christmas, who had walked beyond her husband.

"Mudrick!" shouted Mr Christmas. "Where are you?"

A yawning elf stumbled sleepily into the court-yard, scratched her armpit and rubbed her eyes. When Sealeater saw who was standing in front of her she woke with a start. A look of horror flashed across her face. Then she turned and ran away as fast as she could, slipping and bouncing off the frozen water butt.

"Was that elf wearing what I think she was wearing?" gasped Mr Christmas. "Trainers and a sweatshirt?"

"Probably just mislaid her lederhosen," joked Mrs Christmas, trying to lighten the atmosphere. But when Dancer staggered past with an empty bottle of vodka upturned on his antler it was clearly not a laughing matter. The reindeer hiccuped and smiled a bleary smile.

"Hello, Mishter Chrishmas," he slurred. "Tiddly-pom! Hic!"

"BOTHER!" exploded Mr Christmas as the reindeer weaved his way between the buildings and headed out towards the fields.

Mr Christmas kicked a crate of empty bottles out of his way and pushed open the door to the factory, but the silence and the cobwebs overwhelmed him. He retreated back into the courtyard passing stacks of tacky toys. Why had Mudrick made so few? There weren't enough presents for *half* the world's children. But worse was still to come. The stables were empty. The straw was damp and musty and the reindeer nowhere to be seen. Dirty bridles, unpolished brass and a cold, unlit forge all served to increase the old man's misery.

Then suddenly, without warning, a voice yelled, "Yow!"

Mr Christmas leapt back in alarm as something squirmed in the straw under his feet.

"You're standing on my hand!" squealed the straw-monster as it sprang into the light with Mudrick's old computer game in its hand.

"Pots?" said Mr Christmas.

"Mr Christmas," replied the jug-eared elf. "Hello."

"What are you doing?" asked the old man.

"I live here," answered Pots. "Oh, Mr Christmas," he went on eagerly, "look what I can do!" He pressed a sequence of buttons on the computer game. A tiny hologram appeared *outside* the screen, like a virtual marionette. It was a hologram of Gandor the Goblin King swirling a sword around his head.

"Mudrick said it was useless and didn't work," said Pots, "but I can make the goblin dance!" He beamed.

Mr Christmas had never seen a computer game before, let alone one that had miraculously come to life – and he suddenly saw the elf through different eyes. Pots was not a harmless fool, but a shy child with an instinct for computers. He was the possessor of a mathematical mind capable of complex three-dimensional abstract thought. In fact, Pots was a genius.

"Why are you living here?" he asked.

"Why am I living here?" said Pots. "Nowhere else to go, Mr Christmas. Nothing else to do. And if I close my eyes I can smell the reindeer and pretend they never went away."

"But I just saw one of them in the courtyard," said Mr Christmas. "They haven't gone away."

To explain what he meant, Pots took his old master by the hand and led him outside to a secret place where they could observe the field behind the factory.

"They're living there now," said the elf. "They've forgotten all about me."

The reindeer's private pleasure park was anything but pleasurable. An air of listlessness pervaded the group, giving the impression that they were both worried and bored at the same time.

"No, it was definitely him and he definitely saw me," Dancer was saying as he swung on the gate with Prancer. "What have I gone and done?"

Nobody replied. Blitzen was sitting on a deck-chair balancing an empty beer can on his nose, Vixen was trying to sleep under a faulty sunlamp, Comet was painting her hooves and Donner was lying on his back watching TV, idly throwing snowballs in the air.

"I'm bored," he groaned, letting a snowball hit him full in the face.

"And I'm fat," sighed Prancer, realizing as he took another bite from his cream cake that he really didn't want it.

Mr Christmas turned away. He helped his wife over a pile of black plastic sacks brimming with party hats and half-chewed turkey bones, and together they entered the cottage.

The kitchen was trashed. It looked like a team of burglars had turned the place over. Furniture was upside down, pictures were skew-whiff and the snapped-off leg of a chair lay smouldering in the ashes of the fire. Mrs Christmas collapsed against her husband's shoulder as their son suddenly appeared, running downstairs and pulling on his clothes at the same time. He slipped down the last few steps and tumbled to the floor. His hair was unbrushed, his face unshaven, and under the scrubby black beard his skin was as pale as a shroud.

"Mum. Dad. You're back!" said Mudrick,

sounding guilty and flustered. "Is it Christmas Eve already? Sorry. We had a bit of a party last night" – he clutched his throbbing head – "and the night before and the night before that. It's been three days solid actually. I think I might have overslept."

Mudrick stopped, conscious that his parents had not moved since his arrival. They had not rushed forward to hug him or give him a kiss. They hadn't even smiled.

"Is something wrong?" he asked, knowing full well that it was.

"What's going on?" said Mr Christmas quietly. In his heart he still believed that Mudrick was intrinsically good and wanted to give him the chance to admit his mistake and apologize. Mudrick, on the other hand, had been dreading this confrontation ever since he'd gone behind his father's back. Now that it was here, there was no point in lying. The evidence was there for all to see, but he believed that if he could just make his parents see how brilliant his idea was, they would forgive him.

"Why don't you sit down?" he said. "Isn't it great?"

"What?" said his father.

"That you can take it easy from now on," he said brightly. Then he added, "It's called fatherchristmas.com, Dad. We're going to be rich!"

Mr Christmas closed his eyes and took a deep breath before saying very slowly and clearly, "I don't want to be rich."

"No, but I do!" squealed Mudrick, rushing to

the door and flinging it open. Word had got around and behind him in the courtyard, the elves and the pie-eyed reindeer waited to speak to their old master. "And so do *they*!"

"No," cried Papagrolin.

"Not I," roared Rudolph.

"We tried to stop him," said Dasher.

But Mr Christmas did not want to hear their excuses. He slammed the door in his old friends' faces and turned on his son.

"It's mutiny!" he hissed.

"Not really," said Mudrick defensively. "Dotcom companies are where the smart money is these days."

"Smart?" snapped his father. "Reducing Christmas to a cheap market stall? You call that smart?" Mrs Christmas sank into a chair. "Buying a present on the Interwhatsit is not the same as waking up and finding a surprise on the end of your bed. The answer's no."

At this Mudrick laughed. "I wasn't asking your permission, Dad," he said. "It's a done deal. I've retired you."

There was an awkward silence while the paint curled off the walls with embarrassment. Then Mr Christmas stood up and walked out of the cottage.

"Have you gone mad?" Mrs Christmas asked her son.

Mr Christmas had left the room to stop himself from hitting Mudrick. He wanted to knock some sense into that misguided brain! But he knew that Mudrick's failure was *his* failure too. Something had to be done urgently to save Christmas, but *what*?

In the courtyard the elves and the reindeer were still waiting, but Mr Christmas was in no mood for a chat. He pushed his way through the crowd and found himself walking past the factory to the generator, where Tank was stoking the furnace. At first Mr Christmas saw nothing wrong, but as he got closer he realized *what* Tank was burning. In a few short strides he was by the elf's side and had knocked the shovel out of his hands. Tank fell backwards under the blow.

"What do you think you're doing?" roared Mr Christmas.

"Making electricity," whimpered Tank, "to keep the computer going. The sooner I burn these letters, the sooner I get home for my dinner."

"Get out of my sight!" exploded the old man.

Tank scrambled away and Mr Christmas scooped a handful of letters off the pile. He read the one on top:

DeaR FatheR ChRistmas,

No pensil case on website yet. And I only want a pensil case. Not doll or otheR Rubbish. Seems theRe iz no point wRiting as you neveR Reply and don't lissen to any think I say.

Bye-bye foR eveR.

Kassalina

103

It broke his heart.

On his way back to the house Mr Christmas bumped into Mudrick, who was rushing to find him.

"There you are. Dad, don't frighten the elves. Tank's only doing what I told him to."

But his father was seething. "With every letter you burn, Mudrick, you destroy a part of the child who wrote it. The part that believes in magic!"

He turned his back on his son and went into the cottage. He walked straight past Mrs Christmas, who was grimly tidying up the mess from the party, and climbed the stairs.

"Theo?" she called. "Theo. Where are you going?"

Mr Christmas stopped, and without turning round said, "I've let the children down, Gertie."

There was a noise in the doorway. It was Mudrick creeping in.

"It's still a good idea," he muttered pathetically. "I mean, at least I tried."

Mr Christmas's shoulders stiffened before he continued his journey upstairs.

Mudrick and his mother stood in awkward silence. Neither knew what to say. Even when there was a loud knock at the door neither moved.

CHAPTER FOURTEEN

When Mudrick finally did open the front door he rather wished he hadn't. Outside in the courtyard stood the reindeer and the elves. There was a businesslike buzz to the crowd. They hadn't come to make polite conversation; they had come to make a point.

"You said it would work," said Dancer, bravely speaking first. There was a slight pause while everyone waited for Mudrick to react. "But what's the point of being magic reindeer if we never get to fly?"

"I agree," mumbled Comet. Then with fading confidence she added, "At least I think I do!"

Donner cleared his throat to let everyone know that he would be speaking next.

"Rudolph once said that the time would come when we'd start missing Christmas. He was right," he said.

"And what's the point of making toys that nobody wants?" shouted Sealeater.

"We've had orders," Mudrick said defensively, putting his arm round Tobin's shoulder to show that he still had friends. "Tell them how many, Tobin."

"One." said Tobin. "The one that was cancelled." Like everyone else Tobin had given up any idea of becoming rich.

"Don't be so miserable," said Mudrick. "It's bound to pick up the nearer we get to Christmas."

"It's already Christmas Eve," said Dasher. "How much nearer does it have to get?"

"It was OK when we thought every child was going to get a present," explained Sealeater, "but now..."

"It's boring!" shouted Dancer. "It's dull dull *dull* doing nothing!"

"And I want my hips back!" cried Prancer.

But Mudrick's confrontation with the quarrelsome crowd in the courtyard was suddenly terminated when the front door was slammed shut in his face. He turned to find himself facing his mother. She had a glint in her eye and a rolling pin in her hand.

"I want a word with you!" she growled in a tone of voice that made Mudrick cower like a frightened child. "It's over, Mudrick. It hasn't worked. You've failed."

Mudrick knew she was right, but he found it hard to accept. His original idea had been so simple – make presents, sell presents, retire to the Bahamas! Where had it all gone wrong?

Suddenly the big computer groaned. There was a white flash and then the screen shut down. Simultaneously there was a shout from outside. The kitchen door burst open and Tank fell into the room.

"Mudrick!" he yelled. "Mudrick! There's nothing left to burn. The furnace has gone out!"

Without a furnace there was no generator. Without a generator there was no power. Without power there was no computer. Without the computer there was no fatherchristmas.com. Without fatherchristmas.com Mudrick looked rather stupid.

She took no pride in it, but Mrs Christmas felt her spirits rising.

Upstairs, Mr Christmas was sitting by the window stroking Custard's ears.

"What are we going to do, old friend?" he said. His fury had dissipated. He was just anxious now. Christmas must be salvaged. That was imperative. Every child needed a present. That was imperative too. But Christmas Day was tomorrow. He had no time to think! He lifted Custard's head and stroked the back of his neck. As he did so, his fingers brushed against the cold metallic name tag on the snow leopard's collar. Mr Christmas stopped stroking and wondered.

Outside in the courtyard Mudrick and his disenchanted workforce were at one another's throats arguing about the best way forward. Tobin had his hand raised.

"This has gone far enough!" he shouted. "We've

stolen Christmas from the children and now we're going to give it back."

"I agree!" cried Sealeater.

"Us too!" hollered Blitzen and Vixen.

"And me!"

"And me!"

"And me!"

One by one the elves and reindeer pledged their support for a return to the old ways.

"So let's put the sleigh back together and give the children the toys we've already made," suggested Tobin.

"We didn't make enough," said Comet.

"Then we'll make some more!" Dasher yelled with youthful enthusiasm.

"We can't," said Tank. "There's no power for the factory."

"Oh, for goodness' sake!" exploded Papagrolin. "It's Christmas! We have to deliver something."

"So what are we going to do?" peeped Prancer.

There was a long silence followed by a squeak of metal. Heads turned to look up at the top floor of the cottage. Standing at the open bedroom window, dressed in a red moth-eaten costume, was an old man with a long white beard.

"I'm back!" said Mr Christmas.

And as he spoke, it started snowing again.

CHAPTER FIFTEEN

Mr Christmas had decided to take the bull by the horns. How did the saying go? "Nothing ever gets done without someone *doing* something first!" Unfortunately time was not on his side. It was already Christmas Eve and there were only eight hours left before normal take-off time. While Mrs Christmas prepared the usual in-flight picnic, Mr Christmas brainstormed ideas with the reindeer, the elves and Mudrick. Deep down Mudrick was glad that his father had stepped in. He couldn't actually bring himself to apologize for the havoc he'd caused, but he was grateful for the chance to be part of the think tank that would find a solution.

"All we've got to do is think of a present that doesn't have to be made," said Mr Christmas, "make more than three billion of them in the next couple of hours and distribute them round the world before daybreak."

"Pots, will you stop fiddling!" shouted Mudrick suddenly. "My dad is trying to think." In the corner Pots was playing gladiators with his tiny hologram goblins, and the click-clack of his fingers on the controls was very irritating.

"Sorry, Mr Mudrick," said Pots, and Mr Christmas smiled indulgently at the jug-eared elf.

"No harm done," he said as Pots vaporized the holograms. Then he went on. "To achieve the impossible I have the help of eight fat reindeer, a rusty sleigh and a clapped-out factory."

"Correct," said Papagrolin, who was trying to sound positive, when in his heart of hearts he knew that this was one delivery they would *never* make.

"Right!" said Mr Christmas, leaping to his feet and rubbing his hands on his beard. "There's work to be done."

The easy things were sorted first. Sealeater and her packers and stackers put the sleigh back together again, polished the runners, gave it a service and beat out the dust from the seats. In an effort to fight the flab the reindeer were put on a crash diet of carrot juice and prunes and flung into a get-fit-quick regime, which involved running on the spot, press-ups, sit-ups, squat crunches and star jumps. Pots polished the brass, oiled the bridles and forged thirty-two magic reindeer shoes with the help of his tiny hologram goblins, who kept the coals hot by jumping up and down on the bellows. All that was left to do was to think up the one perfect present.

Father and son wrestled with all sorts of ideas –
bicycle transfers, diamanté hair grips, shin pads,
pot-pourri cushions, insect collection kits, cookery
cards – but everything they thought of was far too
complicated to make in the short time available.

"I've got it!" yelped Mr Christmas suddenly. "It's
been bugging me for hours. Custard's name tag!"

Mudrick gave his father a sideways glance as if
to say, "Are you losing your marbles?"

Mr Christmas was too carried away to notice.
"You see, you can't give a real present, because there
isn't time to make one. So it has to be a present that
exists, but *doesn't* exist at the same time."

"I think you're making sense," said Mudrick.
"Go on."

"Like a promise," mulled his father. "Or magic!"

"Magic sounds good," said Mudrick.

"We'll give all the children a magic token like
Custard's name tag," said Mr Christmas.

"Why?" asked Mudrick.

"Because it won't be a tag – it'll be the promise of
a present!"

"You'll need a letter explaining how it works,"
said Mudrick thoughtfully.

"A letter … yes!" said his father. "Brilliant! But
no … we'll never write over three billion in time."

"We will on my computer," said Mudrick.

There was a flicker of a pause while they checked
each other out. If Mr Christmas accepted Mudrick's
proposal he would, for the first time ever, be com-
promising his traditions.

"I can live with that," said the man in red.

"I thought you didn't trust computers," said Mudrick.

"So now I can't change my mind?" teased his father. All he had ever wanted was for him and his son to sing from the same song sheet. How strange that it had taken all this pain to make it happen.

"One problem," said Mudrick. "The computer's not working. There's no electricity."

"Then use straw from the stables." The old man smiled. The straw would feed the furnace that would restart the generator that would juice up the factory and boot up the computer for business again!

So while Tank stoked up the furnace with straw, and Mudrick concentrated on writing the letter, Mr Christmas marched Custard, Tobin and Sealeater into the abandoned factory and stood them next to a badge-making machine. The power was restored. Lights flickered back on. Mr Christmas picked up Custard, plonked him on a table and twisted his name tag round so that everyone could see it.

"I want more than three billion of these without the *Custard*," he said. "*Promise* printed on one side. *Magic* on the other."

"No problem," Sealeater said. "Ready in five."

"Minutes?" he asked hopefully.

"Hours," she said.

It was six thirty. Normal take-off time on Christmas Eve was six o'clock sharp. The operation was already running late.

There was no time to draw breath. Mr Christmas

112

dashed back into the kitchen to see how Mudrick was getting on with the letter.

"Is it done?" he asked.

"You tell me," said Mudrick. "You're the boss."

Mrs Christmas looked up from making her bloater paste sandwiches and smiled. It was good to hear Mudrick calling his dad "boss"!

I PROMISE TO PAY THE BEARER OF THIS LETTER SOME REAL MAGIC

Dear child,

Sorry for the mess-up this year, but I hope this unusual present makes up for it. It's a magic sleigh ride! Please return the slip below (just post it up your chimney) stating name, date, time and place of pick-up. Then, at the allotted time, wear the Promise Magic badge that is pinned to this letter and I shall whisk you off in less than a trice on a round-the-world trip in my magic sleigh! Don't worry about Rudolph and his reindeer getting tired. They've got magic hooves. Besides, they're too plump and a little bit of exercise will do them good!

Back to normal next year! Up, up and away!

Father Christmas

✂---

Name: _____

Date of Pick-Up: _____

Time of Pick-Up: _____

Address: _____

Mr Christmas was happy and gave Mudrick the go-ahead to print out more than three billion copies. That meant that everything was now in order … everything except the time! The badges wouldn't be finished much before midnight. How was he going to squeeze a twelve-hour journey into six?

"Dad," said Mudrick. "Would you like to hear my other idea?"

Mr Christmas was not sure. Mudrick's ideas had a way of going wrong.

"I don't know," he said. "Would I?"

"I think so," said Mudrick. "We could use the computer to streamline the present drop. We could program it to work out a new route that stops at every child's house, but makes sure that you only travel round the world once. It'll save you hours."

Mr Christmas was awe-struck. "So I could leave at midnight and still get it all done?"

"In theory," said the boy.

"Mudrick," cried his father. "You may just have saved our bacon!"

"No, wait," said Mudrick, holding up a hand to calm his father down. "There is a drawback. I can't program a computer. Hamblatt and Poochie are just designers. We need a high-tech whizz-kid. And how many of those are there at the North Pole?"

It was Mr Christmas's turn to spring a surprise. "One," he said casually. "Pots! Get in here now!"

"Not Pots!" exclaimed Mudrick. "I know he's kind and loyal, but he's not exactly blessed with brains, is he?"

"Isn't he?" said Mr Christmas. "Let's find out, shall we?"

A cloud of soot mushroomed out of the chimney as Pots tumbled across the hearth with a thump, rattle and roll.

"Mr Christmas," coughed the jug-eared elf, "you called."

"What were you doing in the chimney, Pots?" asked Mudrick.

"I wasn't in the chimney pots. I was in the chimney," said the elf.

"There's no time for arguing," barked Mr Christmas. "Now here's the thing, Pots. Can you streamline the present drop using that computer?"

The elf smiled. "I did think of offering to do it earlier," he said, "but I didn't want to be the voice of doom, Mr Christmas, telling you that you would be the most hated man in the whole history of the world if you didn't deliver the presents tonight, and that if you *didn't* leave till midnight and *did* follow your traditional route, you wouldn't."

"Sorry?" said Mr Christmas. "Can you do it or not?"

"With a little help from my friends." Pots beamed as he flicked a switch on Mudrick's old computer game, conjuring up his midget holograms and making them dance.

So while the letters printed out and Mr Christmas busied himself in the corner stitching a cylindrical case from a small piece of leather (he wouldn't tell anyone what he was doing), Pots sat down at the

115

computer and wove his own special magic. He took all of the names of all of the children in all of the world from the Present Ledger (not forgetting Abelard Affleck), and typed them into the computer along with all of their addresses. He had help, of course, from the goblin holograms, whose little fingers tapped faster than any machine. Within an hour they had entered the names and written the program, and within two hours the big computer had worked out a new delivery route that would save Father Christmas five hours and fifty-nine minutes of flying time!

The old wooden clock struck midnight as Mr Christmas lifted his hat and coat off the hook on the back of the door and kissed his wife goodbye.

"Happy Christmas, Gertie," he said. "Time to go."

Then she handed him his packed dinner and he left the cottage for the snowfield, where the magic sleigh was loaded up and raring to go.

CHAPTER SIXTEEN

Papagrolin was standing in front of the sleigh holding up the long wooden yoke with its four padded crossbars.

"Right," he asked the reindeer, "who's going up the front?"

For a split second nobody moved. It looked as if nothing had changed. Rudolph and Dasher always led – why should this year be any different? Then Blitzen raised a hoof and Vixen stepped forward to join him.

"Would anyone mind if we did?" she asked.

Rudolph and Dasher sighed with relief and shook their heads.

"Be our guests!" said Dasher. "We'll cadge a nice cushy ride at the back!"

A few seconds later, Mr Christmas arrived carrying his new route-map. With a quick wave to the elves he climbed aboard the sleigh and started the launch procedure.

"Pots! Fire up the talismanic motor!" he cried.

"Pots?" But Pots was nowhere to be seen. "Bother," exclaimed the old man. Without the talismanic motor there could be no trip.

"I'll start it for a bag of crisps!" shouted a voice in the crowd.

"Oh, very well, Tank," said Mr Christmas, chucking his crisps at the giant elf, "but get a move on."

Unfortunately Tank did not know his own strength. He tugged so hard that the starter cord snapped.

"What have you done!" wailed Mr Christmas. "Now the sleigh will never fly."

Tank wanted the earth to swallow him up.

"Stand back!" cried a voice in the crowd. "Mechanic coming through!"

It was Pots staggering to the rescue. Seeing what had happened, he'd quickly nailed a dozen reindeer shoes to the bottom of his boots. To an appreciative roar from the crowd he stumbled over to the sleigh and gave the talismanic motor one almighty kick. It burst into life, spreading its warm purple glow across the snow.

"Bravo!" laughed Mr Christmas to excited cheers from the crowd. "Pots for president!"

The jug-eared elf blushed scarlet with pride.

"You left this on the table," he said, handing over the little hand-stitched leather case.

"I don't know what I'd do without you, Pots!"

The old man chuckled.

Pots blushed an ever deeper red. "Mr Christmas," he said, pointing at the case. "What is it?"

"Just a little something for someone special," answered Mr Christmas. "And please call me Theo."

"Good luck, Theo!" cried the crowd spontaneously.

It was time to go, but before the sleigh could take off Mr Christmas had one last duty to perform. He stood on his seat and held up Pots's computerized route-map.

"I need a volunteer to map-read," he said.

Tobin smiled ruefully. It was time for another ride in the spew-master! Or maybe not, because someone else had their hand up.

"Mudrick!" Mr Christmas beamed. "I rather hoped it might be you." He beckoned his son forward. "I've got one or two things I want to teach you, young man."

Mudrick made his way towards the sleigh while Rudolph had a quiet word with the boss.

"Does this mean we're not flying alphabetically this year?" he asked.

"That's right," whispered Mr Christmas. "Don't tell anyone, Rudolph, but I was wrong!"

Mudrick stepped into the sleigh and gave his father a hug. "I'm sorry, Dad," he said softly.

Mr Christmas smiled and choked back a tear. "You will be if we don't deliver these presents on time!" he roared. Then, with the crowd's final cheer

119

ringing in their ears, off they flew, father and son, side by side, to the stars and beyond.

"Is it just me or is there magic in the air again?" asked Mudrick.

"No," said Mr Christmas. "No, Mudrick. It's not just you!"

CHAPTER SEVENTEEN

Name: __Kassalina Boto__

Date of Pick-Up: __27 JanuaRy__

Time of Pick-Up: __3.45 p.m.__

Address: __My House, Mbale, Uganda__

DeaR FatheR ChRistmas,

I new you wos Real! Thank you,
thank you, thank you, thank you for
my leather pensil case which did
fell out of the sky last night while
I was asleeping. And wen I did
wake up theRe it was by magic. It
is the most bewtiful leather pensil
case in the wuRld and now I have
lots of fRends and am whole giRl
agen.

C U on 27 JanuaRy and agen
next yeaR.

Love

Kassalina

When the world woke up on Christmas Day there
was indeed magic in the air, especially for a little girl
in Uganda. As the weeks wore on Mr Christmas
received billions of replies to his letter as children
booked their rides on the magic sleigh. It turned out
to be a busy year with all the rides to organize, but
Mudrick, Pots and the big computer coped effort-
lessly with the increased workload. And Pots did not
stop there. He streamlined the entire operation:

the making of toys, the packing, the checking, the answering of letters. After six months the first elves were able to take a well-deserved holiday – Tobin and Papagrolin swam with the dolphins in Florida. Very soon elves were taking holidays all over the world and coming home happy to go back to work. The reindeer weren't forgotten either. Mr Christmas bought them a brand-new wide-screen television. He said it was so they could watch horse racing, but secretly everyone knew it was so *he* could watch *Countdown*.

As the year went by, even Mr Christmas had the odd day off. He flew Mrs Christmas and Custard to Herne Bay, where they played bowls till sunset. On these days a substitute Father Christmas took over the reins and ran the magic sleigh rides. Only this Father Christmas had a beard that was black and an L-plate on the back of the sleigh.

"Name's Mudrick," the sleigh driver told the children. "I'm Father Christmas's son."

In recognition of Mr Christmas's achievement – successfully combining computer technology with traditional work practices – the British government (still New Labour) rebranded Father Christmas New Father Christmas. But, like Mudrick's botched attempt at taking over, the new name meant nothing to anyone and didn't stick. Some people never learn.

JOHNNY CASANOVA
Jamie Rix

Johnny Worms is hot to trot, the unstoppable sex machine, Johnny Casanova.

Well, so he believes. His best friend, Ginger, may tell him that "girls is trouble", but when love's thunderbolt strikes in the form of Alison Mallinson or a beautiful vision in purple, what can Johnny do? Is it his fault he's irresistible?

"Genuinely funny … sparkingly well-written." *The Independent*

"Hilariously funny." *The Times*

THE CHANGING FACE OF
JOHNNY CASANOVA
Jamie Rix

Johnny Worms, alias Johnny Casanova, is back on the luv trail!

A year older, a year ... hairier, meet the all-new all-manly Johnny Casanova. He's got hordes of have-a-go hormones and he doesn't wear pyjamas! He could do without the spots though, especially when gorgeous Bosie Cricket cartwheels into his life and puts his heart in a spin. Could it be he'll finally get a snog?

"Glorious... This book is terrific. More, please."
Adèle Geras, TES

"It's like Adrian Mole but dafter... You'll luv it!"
The Times